NO HIDING PLACE

M A COMLEY

This book is dedicated to the one person who has stood by me through thick and thin throughout my life, my beautiful Mother, Jean.

I'd also like to dedicate this book to the wonderful John Dunne, who sadly passed away just before this book was completed. R.I.P. John. My sincere condolences go to his loving Mum, Lesley, and my dear friend, Audrey Gibson. May the special times you shared with John before his premature departure, dwarf the amount of grief you're experiencing at this sad time, ladies.

Special thanks as always go to my talented editor Stefanic Spangler Buswell and to Karri Klawiter for her cover design expertise.

My heartfelt thanks go to my superb beta reader Mary Endersbe, and my wonderful proofreaders, Joseph Calleja, Tara Lyons, and Irene, for spotting all the lingering nits. You guys rock.

New York Times and USA Today bestselling author M A
Comley
Published by Jeamel Publishing limited
Copyright © 2015 M A Comley
Digital Edition, License Notes

ISBN-13:978-1517748104

ISBN-10:1517748100

OTHER BOOKS BY
M A COMLEY
Blind Justice
Cruel Justice
Impeding Justice
Final Justice
Foul Justice
Guaranteed Justice
Ultimate Justice
Virtual Justice
Hostile Justice
Tortured Justice
Rough Justice
Dubious Justice
Calculated Justice
Twisted Justice (Due out December 2015)
Forever Watching You
Wrong Place (DI Sally Parker thriller)
No Hiding Place (DI Sally Parker thriller)
Evil In Disguise – Based on True events novel
Deadly Act (Hero series novella)
Torn Apart (Hero Series #1)
End Result (Hero Series #2)
Sole Intention (Intention Series #1)
Grave Intention (Intention Series #2)
Merry Widow (A Lorne Simpkins short story)
It's A Dog's Life (A Lorne Simpkins short story)
A Time To Heal (A Sweet Romance)
A Time For Change (A Sweet Romance)
High Spirits
The Temptation Series (Romantic Suspense/New Adult
Novellas)
Past Temptation (available now)
Lost Temptation (available now)
Keep in touch with the author at
http://www.facebook.com/pages/Mel-Comley/264745836884860
http://melcomley.blogspot.com
http://melcomleyromances.blogspot.com
Subscribe to newsletter

No Hiding Place

Prologue

Despite the cooler evenings emerging in Norfolk, the pub where Gemma and her friends were chilling out had become hot and sticky.

"Listen, I'm going to step outside for a breath of fresh air. I won't be long," she told her friends.

Audrey eyed her suspiciously and glanced sideways at the man standing at the bar who'd been studying her best friend with interest all evening. "Hmm... are you sure you two haven't been using telepathy?"

Gemma screwed up her nose in disgust. "Eww... you've got to be winding me up. I'm a married woman." She flashed her ring at her friend.

"Like that has stopped you in the past," Audrey ribbed her.

Gemma shook her head, tutted, and picked up her handbag. She knew Audrey was only joking about her being unfaithful to her husband, Mark, in the past, but it didn't stop her wanting to deck her friend for making her out to be a slapper in front of the rest of the group. Still, that was Audrey to a *T*. She always spoke first and thought about the destruction her actions caused later. Gemma made a note to have a chat with her loose-tongued friend on the way home. *With friends like you, matey!*

After nipping to the toilet, Gemma ventured outside to the pub's family area, which thankfully, was free of screaming kids at this time of night. She sat down on one of the swings and imagined her five-year-old daughter, Samantha, climbing the wooden steps to the little house where the slide began and gliding down to the bottom. She loved that child so much it hurt at times. A smile settled on her face as she smoked her cigarette, finally cooling down under the dark star-filled sky and the subtle evening breeze.

Life was good. At least it would be this time next week. Her smile broadened at the thought of what lay ahead of her; she'd made a life-changing decision that would cause her much elation while disappointing others in her life. But that was the nitty-gritty of the unenviable scenario she'd found herself thrust into—it was her life. Losing one of her friends to breast cancer a few months earlier had made her step back and re-evaluate her life and the miserable direction it was heading in. She deserved better. Samantha deserved better. Melinda had been the strongest person Gemma had ever met in her relatively short life. The way she'd handled her illness with dignity and determination right up until her last breath was an inspiration. Melinda had declined further treatment against the wishes of her doctors after she decided the pain and discomfort were no longer worth fighting. She'd slipped away peacefully when the time presented itself, much earlier than her friends had anticipated.

Gemma's eyes misted over as Melinda's beautiful face entered her mind. Gemma had no doubt she would miss her dearly for years to come. That included missing Melinda's daily telephone calls, enquiring how her goddaughter was getting on at her new school. But most of all, she would miss Melinda's willingness to listen without ever judging her. Gemma's other friends seemed to be incapable of doing that. They all had their different qualities and faults, but no one would ever come close to filling Melinda's patient, wonderfully caring, and astute shoes.

She jumped when someone sat on the bench next to her and coughed. Her hand covered her cleavage. "Gosh, you scared the crap out of me."

"I'm sorry. You were in a world of your own there." The man, who had a gentle face, was neither handsome nor ugly, just ordinary looking. His blond hair glinted in the moonlight, creating an ethereal glow around his head.

"I was merely contemplating life. You tend to do that when you lose someone special, I guess."

"That's sad. A close relative?"

"No. One of my best friends. We met at primary school. I actually can't remember a day when I didn't have any contact with her either in person or over the phone. That's why it's so hard."

"You seem to be enjoying yourself with your friends inside, though. Or is that just a smokescreen?"

"I am. Don't get me wrong—I'm sad, but I know that life must go on, all the same. Melinda has left a lasting legacy in the lives she touched during her time on this earth." She held out her hand for the man to shake. "I'm Gemma, by the way."

He took her hand and shook it lightly. "Pleased to meet you, Gemma. I'm Taylor Hew."

"Taylor? That's an unusual name."

He laughed. "Yeah, don't ever tell my mother you think that if you ever have the misfortune of meeting her. She loves it, even if I don't."

Gemma sniggered. "Makes you wonder what our parents were thinking when they named us, right?"

"Indeed. You seem a wise woman, Gemma."

"Crikey, not sure anyone has ever laid that trait at my door before. Maybe I am getting a little wiser as I get older. Who knows?"

"What kind of job do you have?" He raised his hand in front of him. "Tell me to mind my own business if you want."

"No, that's fine. I'm… well, sort of in between jobs at the moment."

"That's a shame. Okay, what career have you had in the past then?"

"Well, before my daughter was born, I was a PA to the director of a local business. I had to give up my job as they couldn't afford to pay maternity leave and employ someone to fill my position at the same time."

"Isn't that illegal? I mean, for them to force you out like that?"

"I didn't really think about it at the time. They offered me a great package, and I found it hard to turn down, so grabbed it with both hands. It wasn't until I'd had my daughter and wanted to return to work that I realised what a fool I'd been. Jobs are so much harder to come by now—*good* jobs, that is."

"I agree. I'm into property developing—boring, I know, but it pays the mortgage and allows me to drive around in that thing." He thumbed over his shoulder towards a few cars parked in the car park.

Feeling devilish, Gemma chuckled and widened her eyes. "Wow, I can't imagine you fitting into that Mini."

His head snapped around. "Ha, ha! I mean the Porsche."

"Oops, silly me. I'm not really interested in cars. Mind you, I would say that, driving around in my old banger. One of these days, I think it's going to let me down badly."

"To be honest, before I got my hands on that beauty, I felt pretty much the same way as you do about cars. Funny how one's perception changes once you have the funds to alter things."

Gemma couldn't have put it better herself. She had been telling herself the same thing for months, hoping to find a way of changing her mundane life, constantly carrying out her daily chores, uttering the words "If only…"

He clicked his fingers to gain her attention. "Hello, Gemma. You've drifted off again."

She shook her head and smiled. "Sorry. Look, it's been lovely talking to you." She rubbed her bare arms. "It's getting a little nippy out here now, and my friends will be thinking I've deserted them. I better rejoin them. It was lovely meeting you." She rose from the bench.

He stood up too and held out his hand for her to shake. He gripped her dainty hand with both of his and held on to it longer than was necessary. "It's been a pleasure getting to know you, Gemma."

She blushed, swiftly withdrew her hand, and hurried inside the pub again. Shivering slightly as she reached the door, she turned to look over her shoulder to see the man still watching her. *Idiot! He could have been a serial killer for all I know. I'm too bloody trusting at times.*

"Here she is! I thought you'd gone home," Audrey complained when Gemma sat down at the table surrounded by four of her friends.

"Sorry, I got chatting to someone and forgot the time. What have I missed?"

Audrey's eyes widened in expectation. "Never mind about that. Chatting to whom?" She looked over at the bar then tapped the side of her nose. "I think I have an inkling."

Gemma's brow furrowed. "You do?"

Audrey pointed. "There was a chap standing at the bar. He's been eyeing you up all evening. I hadn't noticed, but he's gone now. Did he follow you out to the beer garden?"

"I'm not sure. I was sitting in the children's play area, and a man joined me. I can't say I'd taken much notice of him before I laid eyes on him outside. He seemed nice enough."

"What did you chat about?" Audrey asked.

"This and that, nothing special. Although I did get a little maudlin when he caught me thinking about Melinda, it's hard not to."

Audrey reached out and squeezed her hand. "We're all missing her, sweetheart. Granted, probably not as much as you. However, tonight is about celebrating Melinda's life and all that she stood for, right?"

The group of girls raised their glasses and clinked them together over the middle of the table.

"To Melinda. May her soul rest in peace, and may her spirit live long in our minds and our hearts," Gemma said before her throat closed over and her eyes welled up with tears once more.

Audrey nudged her elbow. "She wouldn't appreciate you getting upset, love. Come on, think of all the happy times we've shared over the years."

They spent the next half an hour giggling while sharing affectionate anecdotes about their dear friend, until the last-orders bell rang. Gemma finished her orange juice, hugged all her friends goodbye, then headed for her car. Something made her search the car park for Taylor's Porsche, but it was nowhere to be seen. Her heart sank a little, and she chastised herself for being so disappointed.

On her way home, she contemplated picking up the hitchhiker hoping for a lift, but she knew how foolish that would be, given the time of night. A fast car overtook her and sped past before she could get a glimpse of the driver. A few more cars passed her on the opposite side of the road, almost blinding her when they forgot to dip their headlights as they loomed closer. *Damn idiots! Obviously, people forget about their highway code and the courtesy it teaches once they've passed their bloody driving test.* A car approached from behind and stayed annoyingly close to her rear bumper until she indicated and turned right into the lane that led to her home. She glanced in the rear-view mirror, willing the vehicle to carry on the main road, but her heart sank when the car remained within a few feet of hers.

She swallowed hard. "Please, go away. You're too close to me. If a fox ran out in front of the car, forcing me to slam on the brakes, you'd be up my arse in an instant. Back off, buster."

Her protest proved pointless. The car continued to follow her down the twisty lane. She actually closed her eyes, preparing herself for the impact. When she reopened them to look in her rear-view mirror and saw the headlights of the car following her disappear, meaning they were probably only inches from the rear of her car, she yelled, "Back off!"

Gemma rounded the next corner, fearful of what the next two miles held for her until she reached the ultimate safety of her home. That's when the driver made his move. She grunted as the car shunted her old banger up the rear. "Leave me alone, *damn you.* Are you that eager to get past on the narrow lane?" She decided to brake and pulled into the hedge as far as she could, willing to risk the damage the bramble thorns would do to her paintwork, to let the vehicle pass. When the car stopped behind her, her heart skipped several beats, and she grated through the gears in her haste to get some distance between the two vehicles.

The second she pulled away, she realised the other car had damaged the rear of her banger when the exhaust spewed a puff of smoke. "Damn and blast," she shouted as the car limped along. Another shunt from behind forced her back into the hedgerow. "That's it, buster! Now you're going to get a mouthful. You can't treat people like this." Gemma yanked on the handbrake. She left the car running and hopped out of the vehicle to give the driver a piece of her mind. Another large plume of smoke erupted from her sad car as she reached the rear. She saw the outline of a figure leave the other car and come at her with something raised in the air. The first blow from the metal bar struck her across the face; she fell against her car, dazed. She had the presence of mind to raise a hand to cover her face from yet another strike. But the second blow struck her legs instead of her upper body as she'd expected. Her thin legs crumpled beneath her. Pain surged through every muscle in her body as she lay on the ground, bathed in the headlights of the attacker's car. She stared up at the person striking her. "Please, please don't do this. I have a child I need to care for. If it's money you need, I think I have a tenner in my purse—take it." The blows rained down on her, increasing in intensity the more she screamed out. She was powerless to avoid them. Every blow sucked another inch of her life into a black abyss. Blood ran from her wounds, hot and sticky. *Why? What have I ever done to deserve this? I have everything to live for. My life should be just beginning, not ending...*

CHAPTER ONE

The claustrophobic atmosphere of the tiny flat was beginning to overwhelm Sally. She needed to seriously consider moving on. Rushing into the lounge, she stubbed her toe on the dining chair she'd forgotten to tuck under the table. That was the problem with this place: if she didn't keep on top of tidying things away once she'd used them, they had a tendency of exacting their revenge when she least expected it.

After pouring coffee into a thermos cup, she drove to Wymondham Police Station to begin her day as a Detective Inspector of the Norfolk Constabulary, unsure what kind of day lay ahead of her. Recently, her team had solved a mixed bag of cases, anything from a serial killer on the loose to arresting a car-ringing operation in a sleepy village on the Norfolk-Suffolk border.

Sally contemplated the direction her life was heading as Darryl, her abusive ex-husband, awaited trial. The deed of actually getting her partner, Jack, to arrest Darryl for assaulting her had been a bittersweet experience. On the one hand, she'd gained immense satisfaction from wiping the smug look off his face when Jack had slapped the cuffs on him. However, the thought of having to go to court and give evidence against him filled her with terror. The court date had been set and was only a few weeks away, and the old feelings of doubt had begun seeping into her mind. She could totally empathise with other abused victims caught up in a similar dilemma—it ate away at her and filled every waking minute of her day; at least it would have if Sally hadn't had the strength to push the thought aside in order to carry out her job every day.

She arrived at the station and stepped out of the car as her partner drew up beside her. "Morning, Jack. Good barbecue last night?"

He smiled and locked his car. "It was, actually. I even managed to stay sober this time to enjoy it."

They walked into the station, Sally keyed in her security number, and they both entered the inner sanctum that would be their cosy home for roughly the next eight hours. "That's a bloody miracle for you. How's Teresa doing? She must be getting big now. When's the baby due?"

"She's a bit temperamental at the moment. We can blame that on her hormones, I suppose. The baby is due to make an appearance late October, so about four weeks from now."

"That'll soon be upon us."

As he and Sally climbed the stairs to the first-floor incident room, Jack said, "The docs have hinted that she might need a C-section, not sure she'll be properly formed enough to have a traditional birth."

Sally winced. "Ugh... too much information, matey. Especially for someone who has never had the inclination to have children."

"Why is that?" Jack asked.

Sally turned to look at him. It was unusual for her partner to ask such a personal question of her. "Gosh, now you've put me on the spot. Would you believe me when I say I don't feel as though I've got a maternal bone in my body?"

He exhaled a large breath that puffed out his cheeks and nodded. "I can totally understand that, from a male perspective anyway."

She frowned and asked with a straight face, "Are you saying I'm *masculine?*"

His mouth opened and shut a few times as though he were imitating a goldfish taking in air, as he quickly searched to find a suitable response.

She dug him in the ribs with her elbow as they pushed open the incident room doors and walked through them. "I was joking. Your face is a picture!"

He growled. "Well, I've seen the damage you can do to people who offend you."

She winked and pointed a finger at him. "You'd be wise to remember that in the future before trying to wind me up." Turning to the members of the team already seated at their desks, she asked, "Where are we? Anything new developed overnight?"

The team bade her good morning. Then Detective Constable Joanna Tryst pushed back her chair and approached Sally, carrying a sheet of paper.

"What's this?" Sally tilted her head to the side.

"A new case, boss."

Sally read the details aloud so her partner could hear. "A woman's body was found near Easton, just off the A47, around seven this morning by someone on their way into work. Do we know how long the body had been lying there before it was discovered? Silly question, I'll ask the pathologist when we get there. I take it the Scenes of Crime Officers are already at the location, Joanna."

"They are indeed. That's all the info I can give you anyway, boss."

"You ready to take off, Jack?"

He shrugged. "Might as well get it over with. Do we know how the woman died? Hit and run or something else?"

"Not sure, is the honest answer, sir," Joanna replied with a shrug.

"Okay, not to worry. We'll shoot over there and get the investigation started. Carry on clearing up the backlog of paperwork from the recent cases we've solved, chaps and chapesses, until we return."

Sally and Jack rushed out of the building and drove the fifteen-minute journey in relative silence. When they arrived, the crime scene situated on the country lane had been sectioned off, and uniformed police already onsite had set up a detour. Sally nodded at the police constable who smiled and lifted the tape for her and Jack to duck under.

Simon Bracknall, the local pathologist, was already there, assessing the scene and organising his team.

"Hello, Simon. Can you share any info yet?" Sally asked, smiling.

He turned to look at her and, with a twinkle in his brown eyes, said, "I think we're dealing with a murder."

"Really? What gives you that idea?" she asked, her question laced with sarcasm, as she studied the amount of blood surrounding the victim's corpse.

"Let's get this marquee erected ASAP, lads. Looks likely we'll have a downpour soon."

"All right if I take a closer look?"

"Sure." Simon crouched alongside Sally and pointed to the indents in the young woman's skull.

"Ouch! Can you tell how many times she was struck?"

Simon tutted. "A rough guesstimate would be a dozen or so."

"So, this was an intentional attack, not just a spur-of-the-moment attempt, like to mug her or to hijack her car?"

"Obviously not, because the victim's car and handbag are still here."

"Thanks for pointing that out. It's still early in the day for me." She groaned inwardly at the pathologist's swift putdown.

"You're welcome." He stood and strolled over to the victim's vehicle. "My take on the scene is that someone rammed the car from behind and forced her off the road."

"Crap, why didn't she keep on driving? Why did she pull over and get out of the vehicle?"

"Good questions that we need to find the answers to, Inspector."

Sally nodded. "Any idea what the time of death was?"

"Well, the body was discovered around seven this morning by the gentleman over there." He pointed to a man sitting in his car, looking bewildered. "I'm inclined to think this took place around midnight. Of course, I won't be able to give you a definitive answer until I've carried out a full examination on the body back at the lab."

"I'll have a word with him in a moment. Do you think she was killed instantly? What I'm getting at is, do you think she suffered before she passed?"

"After receiving quite a few blows to the head, I think her life would have been extinguished pretty swiftly. I hope so for her sake. Otherwise, she would've suffered a slow, lingering death. I'm happy to go with the first assumption in this case. Let's concentrate on getting the body covered, and then I'll be able to give you a proper summary of what we're dealing with."

"Thanks. I'll wait over there with my partner. Hang on a sec—did you say the woman had ID on her?"

Simon walked to the back of his van and held out a plastic evidence bag, which contained the woman's small handbag. He withdrew the contents with his gloved hand and opened the woman's driving licence. "Gemma Whiting. Looks like she was a short distance from home, as her address is on this road, farther up this way, towards the village."

Sally motioned for Jack to take down the information, which they would chase up as soon as Simon gave them the low-down on the victim's demise. "Get on to the station, Jack, see if we can get a head start on things, like if the victim was married, that sort of thing."

"Will do." Jack found a quiet area away from the hustle and bustle and rang the station.

Sally returned to the victim and shook her head. "Why? What secrets are you hiding, young lady?"

"Secrets?" Simon asked, looking puzzled. "What makes you think that she has any secrets?"

"Come now, Simon; it's an easy assumption to make, considering the force of the attack she has sustained, in my experience anyway."

"Maybe you're right. It does seem to be a very personal kind of attack and with the added scenario that neither her car nor her bag was removed from the scene."

"Well, I'll make sure this case is investigated thoroughly, as I always do. No one's life should end in such a despicable way at such a young age."

"Agreed. Here we go. The tent is finally up. Please join me, Inspector."

Simon had always been a very courteous sort of chap, unlike other pathologists Sally had worked with over the eight years she'd been on the force. Most of them, though not all, were so far up their own backsides that it blocked the sun out on a daily basis. Simon was different; maybe his heritage had a lot to do with the way he dealt with people. Being a Scot and a Jew couldn't have made life easy for him.

Jack returned from making his call, and he and Sally followed Simon into the tent. Sally was aware that giving Simon a few minutes of observation and thinking time before she bombarded him with questions was wise. Sally folded her arms and studied the victim. Her heartstrings stretched to the max. The woman, who could have been no more than thirty years old, was slim with wavy chestnut-coloured hair that framed a bloody, contorted face. Sally imagined that the victim had been prettier than the average woman on the street. She appeared to be well-dressed, and her outfit was not at all provocative, so Sally doubted the woman's clothes had contributed to the attack, unlike other recent investigations.

"Okay, let's see what we have. Karen, take some shots before I turn the victim over, will you?" Simon instructed one of his colleagues.

A young Scenes of Crime Officer angled a camera at the body from her position close to the victim's feet and fired off several shots before moving to the woman's head and taking another ten shots or so. Then she nodded at Simon and retreated to continue with her task of collecting evidence of the area a few feet away from the body.

Simon gently pushed the body onto its side and studied the open wound to the rear of the head. "Ouch! I'm surmising this was the fatal blow. To me, the attack was borderline extreme. Her attacker could possibly have been outraged about something."

"It seems impossible to even consider that such brutality would come about from a mere car accident, right?"

"My sentiments exactly. Her face took the brunt of a few blows, too, as if someone was trying to obliterate the woman's beauty."

Sally twisted her head this way and that, observing the injuries, trying to figure out if the victim had tried to ward off the attack. "What about defence wounds, Simon?"

The pathologist rocked the corpse back onto the ground then examined each of the victim's arms. "Nope, nothing."

"So, I'm thinking that she was maybe struck from behind with the first blow and then set upon in a violent and frenzied attack. Am I right?"

Jack coughed slightly. "Is that plausible?"

Sally shrugged. "I don't know. That's what we're trying to ascertain. What are you thinking, Jack?"

"Just that it wouldn't make sense. Look at her position to the car. If her vehicle was shunted from behind and she got out of the car to have a go at the other driver, she wouldn't walk backwards towards the person, would she?"

"Good point. So?"

Jack leaned over to observe the corpse and pointed at the victim's jaw. "What if the first blow was to her jaw? Someone took a swing at her with a heavy object and knocked her off balance then carried on with the attack."

Sally's eyes narrowed as she ran through the scenario in her mind. "If the incident took place around midnight, it would've been pitch-black, right? What if the attacker placed their headlights on full beam, momentarily blinding the victim? She probably didn't even see the weapon before it struck her. That's my best guess anyway."

Simon and Jack both nodded. Simon inspected the jaw closely; it moved freely in his hand. "Broken. I suspect your assumption may be right after all, Inspector."

"Anything else you'd care to share with us before we get off, Simon?"

"Not that I can think of. All the wounds are either head or face related. Wait a minute—there's a faint bruise appearing on her chest, around the heart area."

"Okay. Jack and I are going to shoot off. We'll question the witness and send him on his way then report the death to the victim's family, if that's all right with you?"

"Why wouldn't it be, Inspector? Go. I'll continue with the preliminary exam here and then move the victim to the lab for a PM. Do you want to sit in on that one?"

"Would you mind if I didn't? I'd like to question the family members ASAP."

"No problem with me; you know that. Good luck with your investigation. I'll get my report to you as soon as I can."

Sally and Jack left the tent and headed towards the witness.

The man, still looking shell-shocked, got out of his vehicle when he saw Sally and Jack approaching him.

Sally flashed her warrant card. "DI Sally Parker, and this is my partner, DS Jack Blackman. You are?"

He held out his hand for Sally to shake. "Michael Meldrew. This is such an appalling thing to stumble upon."

"I appreciate that, Mr. Meldrew. I promise not to keep you long. Can you tell us what happened?"

He shook his head. "I set off to work as normal, decided to take the scenic route this morning, never dreaming that I would encounter this. That poor woman."

"Did you see any other vehicles in the area?"

"No, nothing. I never usually do at this time of the morning, to be honest, Inspector."

"Do you recognise the victim? Sorry, her car?" Sally asked, pointing at the victim's vehicle.

"I've seen it around, yes. I couldn't tell you who it belonged to, though. Sorry."

"That's okay. Well, I don't want to hold you up any longer than necessary. Thank you for having the patience to stick around and wait for us. Would it be possible for you to give us an official statement now? Is that convenient for you?"

"Of course. Any help I can give, I will."

"Jack, get the constable to take down the statement, will you?"

Her partner set off to collect the constable. While the constable began taking down the statement, Sally and Jack walked back to the car.

"Poor bloke. Not the most pleasant of things to find en route to work. Looks like we'll have to take the long way round to call in on the family home," Jack observed needlessly as they hopped back in the car.

"It'll add a few miles on the journey, Jack. No great hardship really. Stop being a grouchy grandpa." She chuckled when she saw her partner wince out of the corner of her eye.

"You can go off some people, you know."

CHAPTER TWO

On the trip to the victim's house, Sally instructed Jack to chase up the information about the victim she had requested from Joanna.

Jack reeled off the details as Sally pulled into the drive and parked the car. "Gemma, married to Mark Whiting. He's a butcher."

Sally shot round to face her partner. "Is he now?"

Jack tutted. "That doesn't mean a thing, boss."

"I know. Just winding you up, Jack. Right, let's get this over with."

After Jack rang the bell, they waited a few seconds. Sally flashed her ID at the blond man who answered the door. "Mr. Whiting? I'm DI Sally Parker, and this is my partner, DS Jack Blackman."

"Thank God! Have you found her?"

"Your wife?"

"Of course. I reported her missing last night."

"I think we'd better come in, Mr. Whiting."

He pushed the door back against the wall and allowed them access. Sally and Jack followed the distraught man through the house into a kitchen, where a cute little girl wearing a pink pinafore dress and matching pink shoes was sitting at the table, eating a bowl of cereal. "This little cherub is my daughter, Samantha."

"Sorry, Mr. Whiting, is there any chance we can have this conversation alone? My partner can watch over your daughter."

His agitation showed in the form of a grunt, and his eyes rolled up to the ceiling. However, he relented after a few seconds. "In here." He bent down beside his daughter and held her hand. "Daddy won't be long, sweetheart. The nice policeman will sit with you until I return. All right, pumpkin?"

"Can I talk to him? Mummy always tells me it's not good to talk to strangers, Daddy." The girl's long blonde eyelashes fluttered rapidly as she eagerly awaited her father's reply.

"If the nice policeman wants to talk to you, then yes. In this instance, I'm sure Mummy would allow you to talk to him."

"Oh, goody." Samantha pulled out the chair next to her and patted the cushioned seat with her tiny hand. "Here, sit beside me, Mister. What's your name?"

Jack looked bewildered at the thought of spending time with the chatterbox child, but he succumbed and sat next to the child while Sally left the room with her dad.

Mr. Whiting invited her to take a seat on the sofa as he closed the door to the modern living room, which was spotlessly clean and tidy, considering there was a little one in the house.

"Samantha is a real sweetie. How old is she?"

"She's five. She has her moments, but yes, most of the time she's an adorable little angel. She takes after her mother. What news do you have for me on Gemma, Inspector?"

The man was still standing, his elbow resting on the mantelpiece above the open fire. "Perhaps it would be better if you sat down."

He hesitated for a moment or two then dropped into the leather easy chair on his right, his forearms resting on his thighs and his hands clenched together. "Is she in hospital? Has she been injured in a car crash?"

She found it odd that he would suggest his wife had been in a car crash, then chastised herself for thinking along those lines. *Wouldn't the majority of folks think the same?* She chewed on the inside of her mouth then delivered the news that she feared would rock this man's world for years to come. "I'm sorry, Mr. Whiting. It is regrettable that I have to inform you that Gemma is dead."

His eyes widened, and his mouth hung open. Eventually, he found his voice. "What do you mean she's dead?"

"Again, this is difficult for me to say, but it looks as though your wife was murdered last night."

He jumped to his feet and started to pace the floor. "What? Murdered? Who would do such a thing?" His shaking hand swept over his face and covered his eyes as the tears began to fall. His shoulders shuddered. "My God, who would do such a thing? To Gemma, of all people? She was gentle, compassionate, a beautiful person, and wonderful mother. Jesus, how am I going to tell Samantha that she'll never lay eyes on her mother ever again?"

"Is there someone who can help you with that? What about your parents? Or Gemma's, come to that. I'll need to inform them of Gemma's death."

"They're divorced. She doesn't really see her dad much after he ran off to live with that tart."

The venomous words surprised Sally. "If you give me your mother's phone number, perhaps I could call her for you, ask her to come over and sit with you."

"No, I'll do it. Mum would never forgive me if she heard this news from a stranger."

"I understand. Can you make the call now? Are you up to that?"

He sucked in a large breath and released it slowly through his quivering lips. Then he walked across the room to the side table in the corner and picked up the phone. "Mum, it's me. Something dreadful has happened. Can you come over? No, I can't tell you more than that over the phone. Okay… see you soon."

He hung up and returned to the easy chair. "Mum will be devastated when I tell her. She loved Gemma like a daughter, the daughter she never had. The whole family loved Gemma, in fact."

"What about you? Did you love her, Mark?"

He looked Sally in the eye and shook his head. "How could you even ask such a thing? I've always loved my wife."

"Good, glad to hear it. I had to ask; I'm sorry. We hear about so many cases where husbands and wives have fallen out of love with each other and instead of agreeing to an amicable divorce, one of the spouses does something stupid like ending the other's life."

"Really? What a bloody sad world we live in."

"Indeed. Are you up to answering some questions?"

"Go on. Not sure I'm *compos mentis* enough to answer them fully, so you'll have to forgive me."

"I will. Let's see how we go. Right, I take it your wife went out last night. Can you tell me where?"

"Out with a few of her friends. I don't keep my wife on a chain, tied to the house, Inspector."

His comment caused her to frown. *What a strange thing to say!* She smiled, not letting on that she thought his comment was somewhat out of place.

"Maybe you can let me know the names and addresses of those friends? We'll need to chat to them ASAP, to see how the evening panned out."

He went over to the table in the corner again and withdrew an address book. Sally took her notebook and pen from her jacket pocket. "Fire away."

He reeled off four names accompanied by addresses: Audrey Jones, Tara Metcalfe, Nadine Thornley, and Milly Choudary.

"That's excellent."

Just then, the front door slammed, and a dishevelled woman in her early sixties burst into the room. Mark went to the woman and flung his arms around her. She cuddled him back with a puzzled expression covering her makeup-free face. "Whatever is the matter, child?"

With his face buried in her neck, Mark said, "She's dead, Mum. Gemma is dead."

The woman shot Sally a glance then pushed her son upright. "You're not making sense, son. What do you mean, Gemma is dead?"

Sally stood, tucked her notebook into her pocket, and introduced herself to the woman. "I'm DI Sally Parker from the Norfolk Constabulary. We were called out to a scene not far from here, where your daughter-in-law was found, murdered."

The woman's legs wobbled beneath her, and Mark, momentarily forgetting about his own grief, supported his mother and placed her on the couch.

"Murdered? How? Why?" the woman stammered.

"That, I can't tell you at this moment in time. We think her car was struck from behind and forced into a hedge. Looks like she might have confronted the driver of the vehicle, who possibly attacked her for speaking out, perhaps we're looking at a severe case of road rage. That's my initial assessment anyway."

"Oh my. I'm not sure what to say. Where did it happen?"

"Just up the lane. I take it you got diverted at the top of the road. Sorry, I missed your name," Sally said.

"It's Yvette Whiting. Yes, I was diverted at the top. I had no idea why."

"Why don't we all take a seat? I know it's a difficult time for you both, but I have a few questions I need to ask. The sooner I get the answers, the quicker our investigation can begin. Are you up to answering those questions today?"

Mother and son sat on the couch together, hands clasped around each other's. Mrs. Whiting acted as the spokesperson. "If that's the way it has to be, Inspector, then I suppose we better get on with it. Of course we want the person who did this found as soon as possible. My God, poor, poor Gemma."

Sally dropped into the easy chair, and with her notebook at the ready once again, she asked, "What time did your wife leave the house, Mark?"

He inhaled a large breath and scratched his temple. "I think it was around seven thirty. Yes, it was. She popped her head in Samantha's room while I was reading her a bedtime story."

"Excellent. And you say she was meeting up with the friends you mentioned. Can you tell me where?"

"The Red Lion at Cringleford. I think they were scheduled to meet up around eightish," Mark replied.

"That's great. Obviously, you won't be able to tell me what happened during the evening. I'm hoping her friends will be able to fill in the blanks there. Can you tell me if your wife has spoken about any problems lately? Such as, if she felt someone was following her, that sort of thing?"

The pair exchanged puzzled glances, then Mark shook his head. "No, can't say I remember her mentioning anything along those lines. What about you, Mum?"

Yvette's mouth turned down at the sides as she thought, her gaze searing a spot in the rug in front of the fireplace. After a few seconds' delay, she looked Sally in the eye and said, "No. I can't say I remember her discussing such a thing with me. Is that what you think, Inspector? That Gemma was stalked by a crazed man who ended her life in a country lane?"

Sally wanted to chuckle at the expression *crazed man*. However, she kept her face serious when she responded. "It's definitely an avenue we'll be pursuing. Did your wife work, outside the home I mean, Mr. Whiting?" she asked with a sensitive smile.

"No. She wanted to be at home with Samantha for as long as possible."

"And you were agreeable to that?" Sally asked, looking down at her notebook. Her head shot up when Mrs. Whiting answered her question.

"Yes, he agreed to it, in spite of me offering to care for the child while they both went out to work."

"Mum! Stop it. Now is not the time to start having a go about that."

Sally's eyes narrowed. She sensed there was an ongoing conflict between the pair about childcare issues. "Are you retired, Mrs. Whiting? Only you seem too young for that, if you don't mind me saying."

Yvette smiled, and her cheeks flushed the colour of a ripe cherry. "My husband is of a different generation, Inspector. He has always expected me to be at home, rearing our children. Once my children were grown up, it was nigh impossible for me to obtain a job with no experience other than child-rearing. I was hoping I'd raised my sons to think differently to their father."

Mark withdrew his hands from the safety of his mother's and reclined in the sofa.

Sally decided not to press the issue further for fear that it would cause a wedge between mother and son at a time when they most needed each other's comfort. "Going back to Gemma's night out, did she ring you perhaps during the course of the evening, Mark?"

Mrs. Whiting reclined in the sofa too and folded her arms across her chest.

Sally had a hard time figuring out if she'd upset the woman by changing the subject. The woman eyed her son carefully whilst waiting for him to reply.

"No. There was no need for her to ring me, Inspector. I told her to go out and enjoy herself. This was the first time she'd ventured out with the girls in over a year. Why? Why would anyone take my precious wife from me?"

"We'll find out the answer soon enough, Mark. I'm sorry for asking such dumb questions at this time. It's necessary to build a picture of Gemma from the outset. Would you say she was an outgoing person?"

He frowned. "Are you asking if she flirted with people?"

Sally was taken aback by his sharp retort. "That's not exactly what I meant. I was just asking if she was the type to attract attention, in a group or was she an introvert, happy to tag along with the crowd. That sort of thing."

"Maybe it would be best if you directed that question at her friends and not her husband, Inspector. People show different traits when they are out of view of their loved ones," Yvette said abruptly.

"That's a fair assumption, Mrs. Whiting. I'll be asking her friends the same questions; don't worry."

A knock on the door interrupted Sally's flow. "Come in." Jack poked his head into the room, looking very sheepish. In the distance, Sally could hear the little girl crying. *Shit! What's happened?* The couple she was questioning shot off the sofa and pushed past her partner. "What's going on, Jack?"

"I left the table for a second to get the girl a glass of water. When I turned back, she had toppled out of the chair onto the floor."

"What? Bloody hell, I ask you to do one simple thing…"

He shrugged. "I don't know how it happened, boss. I'm sorry."

"Come on. Let's see if the kid is all right."

They rushed into the kitchen to find Mrs. Whiting holding the crying child, smoothing her hand over the girl's face, wiping away the youngster's tears, and kissing the tip of her nose. Mark appeared out of his depth, standing with his hands thrust deep into the pockets of his jeans, looking relieved that his mother had taken charge of the situation. Sally wondered if grief was playing a major role in his inability to pacify his daughter himself. She was amazed that a mother's instinct to protect always kicked in at times such as this.

Sally wondered if she might have had that same motherly instinct. In her eyes, being in a loving relationship was necessary before she embarked on having a child—and she didn't envisage being in that situation in the near future, if ever, after ending her abusive marriage to Darryl. She shook his smarmy image from her mind and stroked Samantha's arm. "Are you all right now, sweetie? Did you have a nasty fall?"

Sniffling, the girl clung to her grandmother's neck and nodded. "I think so. Can Grandma stay with me?" Samantha shot Jack a distrusting glance.

Sally smiled and rubbed the little girl's arm again. "Of course, sweetie, if that's all right with your grandma."

"It is. Why don't we make some cookies? You like making Daddy his favourite cookies, don't you, precious?"

The girl wriggled out of her grandma's arms and, without answering her grandmother's question, rushed over to the larder unit to pick out the ingredients she needed for the recipe.

Sally smiled at Mrs. Whiting. "We'll continue in the lounge, if that's all right with you?"

"Of course. Take him with you," Yvette said, jabbing a pointed finger in Jack's direction.

"Hey, it wasn't my fault," Jack bit back.

Sally pulled his sleeve and led the way back into the lounge, expecting Mark and Jack to follow her. Once the three of them were seated, she asked Jack to take notes and handed him her notebook and pen.

"Your mother is very good with Samantha, Mark."

Mark nodded. "She idolises her. Samantha is her only grandchild."

"That's code for 'the child is spoilt', yes?" Sally asked with a chuckle.

He smiled wearily. "It is. We'd… I mean, *I'd* be lost without her."

"It's good to know that she'll be there to support you over the coming days. You'll be relying on her strength and help in caring for Samantha, no doubt."

His eyes widened. "God, I never thought of that. I suppose I'll have to give up my job to care for Samantha."

Sally smiled. "Not that I profess to know the ins and outs of caring for a child of Samantha's age, but isn't she at primary school by now?"

"Yes, but she's used to my wife being here when she gets home from school mid-afternoon. I won't be able to do that working the job I have now."

Sally was slightly put out by the fact that a grieving widower was already debating what to do next in regard to sorting out his work and caring for his daughter so soon after being told about his wife's unfortunate death. Nevertheless, she pushed aside her feelings and continued. "Okay, if we can go back to where we left off, your mother answered the question before you got a chance to last time, and so I'll repeat what I said: what sort of person was Gemma? Let me put it another way, perhaps you can tell me how you met and what attracted you to your wife in the first instance?"

Mark reclined in the sofa again and crossed his arms. "Let me see…" A smile pulled at his lips as he contemplated his response. "Well, I suppose she used to be outgoing. The type of woman who stood out on the dance floor, not in a showing-off kind of way. That's where we met, actually. She was with a group of her friends on a hen night, and I was with a group of my mates, out on the pull."

Sally nodded. "So you decided to take a chance with Gemma that night?"

"Yes. I asked her to join me in the last dance of the evening. She made a huge impact on my life that night, so much so that we moved in together within a month of our first date."

"A month? Really? How did that go down with your mother? I imagine she must have been quite protective towards you throughout your childhood."

"She was. I suppose she was shocked to begin with, but then she and Gemma became good friends. Mum always said that Gemma was like the daughter she had never conceived. Mum even helped— actually, she was instrumental—in organising our big day. Gemma and I were both grateful for Mum's input as we were working extra hours to pay for the wedding ourselves."

"Why was that? Isn't that down to the bride's parents to pay for the wedding?"

"It should be, but Gemma's dad went off when she was only three. Her mum struggled to bring Gemma up by herself. Gemma's mum used to work two jobs just to cover the household bills every month."

"I see. What about her father? Surely he paid maintenance?"

"No. He left them high and dry, even went to live in Spain with his new floozy. That's the reason Gemma wanted to stay at home with Samantha. She felt as though she'd missed out growing up. She knew her mother loved her, did everything she could to make up for not having her father around, but Gemma still felt that she missed out a great deal in life. It made her more determined than ever to ensure that Samantha didn't miss out on knowing who her mother was."

"Things were that *bad* during Gemma's childhood?"

"No, don't get me wrong. Her childhood was a very happy one. She just longed to see, and be with, her mother more, rather than be farmed out to neighbours after school. She loved her mother dearly for the personal sacrifices she made in order for Gemma to live in a loving home, to have decent food on the table, and clothes on her back."

"I see. Is her father still alive? Did she have any contact with him?"

Mark's eyes narrowed and started to twitch. "He swans into her life now and again. Mainly when he wants to brag about something. Everything is fine between them for a few months until Ray starts chipping away at her self-esteem."

"Really? In what way?" Sally asked, not quite believing that a father could do that to his own daughter. Maybe she was just lucky in that respect, coming from a loving home, bestowed with an abundance of affection from both of her parents. She had a hard job deciding whom she was closest to. Each of her parents had different qualities, but both of them had always put her needs above their own when she was growing up. Perhaps Sally being an only child had something to do with the way her parents had treated her.

"He's all over her when he first crawls back into her life, pleads with her to forgive him for the way he's treated her over the years, then when he's worked his way into her affections again—*bam.*" Mark clicked his fingers. "That's when his true colours come to the fore, and he just starts criticising everything she does. The last time he visited, they had an almighty row because he slapped Samantha on the legs for being naughty. I came home from work to find Gemma pinning her father to the wall in the kitchen with her hand around his throat. I literally had to drag her off him."

"Sounds like a real charmer. We'll need his address, too."

He opened the address book again, flipped to a specific page, then read out Raymond Lord's home address for Jack to note down.

"What happened to their relationship after that incident?"

"I ended up kicking him out of the house. Gemma was beside herself, not for her sake, but because he'd struck Samantha. She was inconsolable for days. I told her to forget about him. Samantha doesn't need a bully like that in her life."

"Was Gemma abused by her father during her childhood?"

He winced and tutted. "We never really discussed it. Her childhood was always reflected upon as being happier once her father had left the marital home. I have no idea what occurred when he lived with Gemma and her mum, Heather, full time."

"I'll see if I can obtain a better insight into the father-child relationship from her mother when we visit her later."

"Yeah, Heather will be better than me at filling in the gaps in Gemma's past. I'm sorry; my mind is all over the place right now."

"There's no need to apologise. I think we have enough to be going on with for the time being. We'll leave you to care for your daughter. If anything comes to mind that you think we should know about in the next few days, will you contact me?" Sally handed him one of her cards as they all rose from their seats and moved towards the lounge door.

"Of course I will. Thank you, Inspector. Please, find the person who did this to Gemma. I know many cases like this go unsolved for some reason or another, but promise me you'll do your best to find the culprit and bring them to justice for robbing my daughter of her beautiful mother."

"You have my word on that. My team will strive to track the offender down and punish them swiftly."

"That's all I can ask."

He closed the front door quietly once they left. "Crap, I'm sorry about the kid, doubly sorry after what he told us about Gemma's father."

"It's forgotten about, Jack. However, Gemma's father hitting Samantha like that needs urgent investigation. It doesn't sit comfortably with me. While I drive to Heather's house, you ring the station and get one of the guys to run a background check on Raymond Lord. Then, once we've seen Gemma's mother, we'll pay her father a visit. Hopefully, Gemma's mum will be able to fill us in more accurately as to the impact he's had on Gemma's life over the years."

Jack placed the call and instructed Joanna to dig up what she could on the raging father and to get back to them ASAP. He hung up, and out of the corner of her eye, Sally saw her partner shaking his head.

"Are you thinking about the father?" Sally asked.

"Yeah. It bothers me that anyone could treat their family like that."

"Not everyone is a compassionate father like you, Jack. The world is crammed full of nasty men who frequently sow their seed without contemplating the responsibilities they'd be lumbered with. Let's hold fire on the recriminations for now until we get the full story from Gemma's mother, eh?"

"Okay. I suppose Gemma was at least fortunate to have one decent parent in her life."

Sally nodded. "Some people don't even have that honour. It's at times like these, I for one, count myself lucky for having wonderful, caring parents."

"Do you think the father could have done this? Is that where all this is leading?"

"At this point, I don't think we can rule him out. Something is bugging me big time about this case. However, I can't quite figure out what is annoying me. I suppose the most important question I have is, why did Gemma feel the need to get out of her car on a dark country road?"

"Good point. If I was female and I got shunted from behind and was only a few miles from home, I know what I'd do—put the pedal to the metal and get the fuck out of there, sharpish."

"That's exactly what I'd do, too, matey. So why didn't Gemma?"

"Is that why you asked all those questions about her character? I wondered where you were leading with that."

"Partially. I like to look at things from the victim's point of view occasionally, when things don't sit right."

"I had noticed. Not so good when we're dealing with a prostitute murder, but I get your drift, boss. Whatever floats your boat."

His wisecrack earned him a thump in the thigh.

"Hey, at least I *think* about a case," she retorted playfully.

CHAPTER THREE

The mid-terraced house owned by Gemma's mother had no front garden and was situated in a rough part of town.

"Don't forget to lock the car," Jack reminded Sally as they approached the front door.

Sally made a point of showing him she'd pressed the button to lock the vehicle before her partner knocked on the front door of the property.

A woman in her fifties answered the door with a cigarette hanging out of her mouth, grasping her towelling robe at her cleavage.

"Hello. Mrs. Lord?"

"I am. And you are?"

Sally produced her ID and introduced herself and her partner. "Is it possible to come in for a chat?"

The woman's brow creased. "About what?"

"Please, take my word that you'll want to hear what I have to say in private," Sally suggested when a woman carrying shopping bags walked past, visibly straining her ear to hear what they were talking about.

"You better come in." Heather Lord walked backwards a few steps to let them gain entry to the property, then she turned and walked through the first door on her left. "Okay, I'm listening. What's this about? I haven't stolen anything or mouthed off to anyone, not as far as I can remember."

"Why don't we all take a seat?" Sally removed a few catalogues from the sofa and placed them on the floor.

"Sorry about that. I'm sorting out my granddaughter's Christmas presents. I buy them through the catalogue to eke out the payments. Of course, I don't tell my daughter that—she'd hit the roof if she thought I was going into debt just to buy them presents."

Sally swallowed then cleared her throat with a gentle cough. "Your daughter is the reason we're here, actually, Mrs. Lord."

"Why? What's she done wrong? I can't believe Gemma would do anything illegal—not my Gemma." Tears glistened in Heather's eyes, and her hand clutched her robe tighter, making her knuckles turn white.

"I'm sorry to have to tell you that your daughter's body was found first thing this morning."

Heather's head protruded, and her eyes widened in disbelief. "What?" she whispered.

"Jack, please get Mrs. Lord a glass of water from the kitchen." Jack rushed out of the room and returned with a glass, which he offered to Mrs. Lord. While the woman sipped at the clear liquid, Sally thought how best to tell the woman about the circumstances surrounding her daughter's death. "It happened on a country lane close to her home. We're still trying to figure out how the incident occurred. I'm so sorry. We've just come from breaking the news to her husband."

Tears flowed down Mrs. Lord's cheeks like a rampant river. "Why? Was this an accident?"

"At this moment in time, we're working on the theory that this was an intentional act."

"Stop blinding me with police talk, Inspector. Are you saying that my daughter was targeted?"

"Yes, it would appear to be the case. If you're up to answering some questions, I'd appreciate it. If not, then we could come back another time."

"What sort of questions? Surely, you should be out there, hunting down the killer, if you believe this to be a deliberate act."

"I agree with you. Nevertheless, it's important for us to find out a little about the victim first and foremost."

Heather wiped her tears on the back of her hand. Fresh ones quickly replaced them. "What type of things?"

"Mainly, whether you can think of anyone who would deliberately set out to hurt your daughter?"

Heather placed her head in her hands and sobbed openly. Sally and Jack exchanged an awkward glance while she wept.

"My baby. My poor baby. I'll never see her again. It's not right for a child to leave this world before the parents." Her head rose, and she looked Sally in the eye and nodded. "*He* did this!"

Sally shook her head as if trying to stir herself from a daze. "Excuse me. Who did it? At least who do you *believe* is responsible for killing Gemma?"

Her lip curled. "Take your pick."

"You're not making any sense, Heather."

"None of this makes sense to me. She's fallen out with so many of her family members lately, it could be any bloody one of them."

Jack withdrew his notebook.

"Okay, I think you better start giving us some names and the reasons why you think they might be in line for us regarding them as a suspect."

"Do we have to do this now? Am I not allowed to grieve, even for twenty-four hours?"

"If that's what you want, then I'm happy to adhere to your wishes, although I do have to tell you that there is every chance of the suspect taking off, the longer we delay things."

Heather let out a long breath and swept a hand over her colourless cheeks. "You should visit that no-good bloody father of hers first."

Sally nodded—so far, the evidence against him was stacking up, placing him at the summit of their suspect list. "Okay. Who else?"

"Her husband, Mark—I wouldn't discount him, either."

"Why do you say that, Heather? Was the marriage in crisis?" Sally asked, flummoxed by the revelation.

"It's had its moments over the years. Like every marriage in this stratosphere."

"Okay, that's plausible and something we'll eagerly delve into."

"Then there's that smarmy shit of a brother of his."

Sally had the notion that Heather, and not just Gemma, had fallen out with most of Mark's family over the years and was merely venting her anger to combat the loss of her daughter.

"I'm getting the impression that you don't care much for any of these men."

She shrugged and exhaled again. "All I'm doing is helping with your enquiries. I believe these men should be taken into consideration when you're looking at suspects. You'd be foolish to ignore me."

"I appreciate that. Do you want to go into detail as to why we should question these men in connection with the... crime?"

Heather lit a cigarette; her brow creased as she thought about Sally's question. "I would rather wait and grieve a while, but I'm aware that any evidence I give you now will get this vile creature off the streets before they can harm anyone else. I doubt that will happen, though, as their target has already been brought down."

Sally smiled at the woman, appreciating her willingness to be open. "Just take your time. Let us know if you need to take a break, okay?"

Heather inhaled a few more puffs of her cigarette, then started telling them about all of Gemma's father's faults, which were lengthy to the point that Sally wondered if Jack would complain his hand hurt once he'd noted down all the information. Before things got out of hand, Sally interrupted Heather. "Okay, I think we need to narrow this down to actual specifics. I appreciate that he's your ex-husband and that he's your ex for a reason, Heather. The thing is, I need to find a possible motive your ex-husband might have for taking his own daughter's life."

"I understand that, and that's what I'm trying to give you, Inspector. Maybe we should call it a day, if you're not interested in what I have to say about him."

"I'm sorry if that's how it came across. Of course I'm interested in what you have to say. My job is to sift the information into piles of possible grievances on your part as an ex-partner and plausible motives for a father killing his own flesh-and-blood daughter."

"Stop right there. This isn't about me trying to get retribution for the years of suffering that man has subjected me and my daughter to in the past. This is about his relationship with Gemma, the child he wanted me to get rid of as soon as I found out I was pregnant with her."

"I see. And yet you went ahead with the pregnancy?"

"I did. No man has the right to *tell* a woman, with his fists, to get rid of her unborn child."

"I agree with you wholeheartedly," Sally said. She looked sideways at Jack, who fidgeted in his seat and refused to raise his head to look at either of the women. He'd recently gone through the same agonising decision whether to ask his sixteen-year-old daughter to terminate the child she was carrying or not. In the end, the family had compromised and was looking forward to the child being welcomed into the fold in the next few weeks. "Therefore, are you saying that he's never treated or loved Gemma like a daughter?"

"He's had his moments over the years, but always ends up spoiling any trust that he tries to build up between them."

Sally found it hard to understand any father not wanting to be part of his own daughter's life.

"When was the last time Gemma had any contact with her father? Can you tell me that?"

"At the beginning of the year. He showed up at the house drunk one day, begging for forgiveness after neglecting her all these years."

"And did Gemma welcome him with open arms?"

"Foolishly, yes. She usually did. The thing is, I've never set out to deter her from seeing her father. I believe children should be guided in this life to form an opinion of people for themselves. There should be no need to force your feelings upon others. Don't you agree?"

"I do." Sally found it strange that Heather would say such a thing after spending about ten minutes at the start of the interview ripping Gemma's father to shreds. Maybe it was her way of venting her grief and anger or frustration with herself for not forcing her child to think poorly of her own father now that she'd lost her life. "So, this time, they remained on speaking terms. Is that right?"

"No, anything but! She left Samantha with him one day while she went out to the shops. When she returned, Samantha was bawling her eyes out, and she had a huge red mark on her bare leg."

"From what?" Sally asked, sitting forward in her chair.

"I suspect it was from his hand, but Gemma seemed to accept his answer that Samantha fell and banged her leg on the table as she tumbled."

"You didn't, though?"

"No, I didn't. I know the bruises he used to give Gemma during her childhood. At one point, I threatened to hit him with a frying pan. On that occasion, I realised we no longer had a future together and told him the marriage was over and to get out of my house."

"How old was Gemma?"

"Just turned three, I believe."

"And you've struggled to bring her up on your own ever since?"

"Yes. He flitted in and out when guilt played havoc with his heartstrings, but apart from that, he pretty much left us alone while I raised her myself."

"That must have been hard?"

"It was, but I managed it. I couldn't have done it without having the best neighbours around for support, though."

"Mark mentioned that you had to work two jobs, which meant that you saw very little of Gemma."

Heather's head tilted to the side. "Is this your way of telling me that I'm on your suspect list, too, Inspector?"

Sally shook her head vigorously. "Not in the slightest. I asked Mark what sort of character Gemma was, and he gave me a rundown attached to a statement, 'considering what her childhood had been like.' I'm sure he never intended it in a derogatory way, Heather."

"The trouble was I had to work my arse off because her father contributed very little to her upbringing, a pittance really. I took him to court one year. The judge looked down at him and called him 'a sorry excuse of a human being' and raised my maintenance money. Actually, he *doubled* it. I walked out of the courtroom with my solicitor to find my ex waiting on the other side of the road with his new young wife, stripping off and shouting, 'Here, you might as well take the shirt off my back, too.' The solicitor whisked me away and bought me a coffee. My hands were shaking so much, I spilt most of it."

"What a terrible experience for you."

"He's a terrible man, Inspector. The world revolves around him and his infantile universe, I'm afraid, and woe betide anyone who doesn't conform to his way of thinking."

"He sounds a real sweetheart. Going back to the incident with Samantha, can you tell me what the outcome was?"

"Gemma said that she believed her father, but deep down, I don't think she really did. She said it would be better for him to leave and ring when he wanted to visit them again."

"Do you know what Mark said about it?"

"I don't think she ever told him."

"That's a bit awkward. Any idea why she would keep that kind of information from the father of her child?"

"Speaking as a mother, it's what we do sometimes."

"Really?" Out of the corner of her eye, Sally noticed Jack's head rose to look at the woman. "Would you appreciate that kind of info being held back as a father, Jack?"

"No, I would not."

Heather shrugged. "To each their own. The marriage was in trouble. I guess Gemma was more cautious about giving her husband information that could be used against her if they split up."

"I can understand that logic. Was there a danger of Gemma and Mark going their separate ways?"

"Not that I'm aware of. I was there only as a shoulder to cry on at the end of the day, Inspector. Maybe Gemma confided in her friends more about that than in me."

"We'll see what they have to say about that then."

"You do that. Going back to the incident with my granddaughter, I wouldn't put it past Ray to have threatened Samantha."

"What? Threaten a five-year-old? How?"

"You know, 'Keep this a secret between us, or I'll tell Mummy you did this.' He used to do it all the time when we were all together."

"That's appalling. I'm not surprised you kicked him out if that was his game."

"Yeah, he's a real peach. Take my word on that."

"I'm looking forward to meeting him. Okay, I think you've drawn a clear enough picture about Gemma's dad to be going on with. You mentioned Mark's brother—care to enlighten me about what kind of relationship he had with Gemma?"

"Are you insinuating that something might have been going on between them, Inspector?"

"No, not in the slightest. Sorry if it came across that way. I was simply asking why they had a falling out. That is what you suggested earlier, wasn't it?" Sally asked, raising a questioning eyebrow.

"Yes. His name is Colin Whiting. He's a baker. Just lately, I've picked up a bad vibe between them when they were in the same room together. I have no idea what was going on. I tried to get it out of Gemma, but she clammed up. Told me to leave well alone."

"Okay, that doesn't sound too good. And there's no way that they'd ever have a relationship?"

"No, she would have been crazy if she had. He seems very needy to me. Not the type you'd want to encourage to be friends at all."

"Did he visit the family home much? Gemma's home, I mean?"

"Not that often. He used to visit up until recently. That's when I noticed a frosty atmosphere between him and Gemma."

"When did you notice this chill develop exactly?"

Heather contemplated her answer for a few seconds as she lit up another cigarette and swept the back of her hand across her cheeks, wiping away fresh tears. She exhaled a large puff of smoke then said, "Well, we all—the family, that is—turned up for a barbecue back in August. Gemma was in the kitchen, preparing the coleslaw. I walked in to get the cutlery and found them deep in conversation. He had his hand on her arm, gripping it, and his face was close to hers. She seemed scared of him. Neither of them appeared to notice my arrival, and I coughed to get their attention. He let go of her arm swiftly and left the room. I asked Gemma what was going on. Her cheeks coloured up, and she told me everything was all right and that I should forget about it."

"Interesting. Did she ever confide in you what the incident was concerning?"

"No. I tried several times to raise the subject, but she refused to tell me what it was about. I hate secrets, Inspector. My advice would be to dig very deep there, too."

"I intend to, I assure you. Is there anything else you think we should know about regarding the family, Heather?"

Her eyes widened. "I think that's enough for you to be going on with. Isn't it, Inspector?"

Sally and Jack stood and followed Heather into the hallway. At the front door, Sally replied, "Yes, you've been very kind talking to us today, considering the sad news I've given you."

"When can I see her?"

Sally placed her hand on the woman's forearm. "I'll have a word with the pathologist to see if we can arrange that soon. Take care, Heather. We'll do everything we can to bring your daughter's murderer to justice. You have my word on that."

She sniffed and wiped away another tear. "Thank you, Inspector. Please keep me informed."

"We will. I'd suggest you have little or no contact with Mark or his family in the meantime. I know that's going to be difficult, and you'll need to restrain yourself after the information you've divulged today, but please, let us handle them."

Heather nodded and closed the front door behind them.

"Oh, what tangled webs," Jack said once they were back in the car.

"Yes, indeed. Strange that Gemma didn't tell her mother about having her father in a stranglehold, eh?"

"Yeah, that's what I thought. It's all very strange."

"I don't need to look into my crystal ball to know that we're about to untangle a lot of secrets; maybe secrets that some of these folks would rather have gone to the grave with the victim. Let's see what Raymond Lord has to say for himself, shall we?"

CHAPTER FOUR

While Sally drove the twenty-odd miles to the address Heather had given them for Raymond Lord, Jack rang Joanna to see what she had garnered from the background checks.

"Thanks, Joanna. We'll be back after we've visited Gemma's father." Jack hung up and tapped his notebook.

"What did she find out?" Sally asked, turning into Forster Road, where Lord's flat was situated.

"He's been in trouble with us over the years."

"Has he now? Come on, Jack, out with it."

"Mostly petty crimes. A few shoplifting charges, nothing major. But there is an assault charge in there, too."

"On whom?"

"A teenager—he was in his teens as well."

"You say that as though that's an acceptable excuse for his actions, partner."

Jack shrugged as she parked the car outside a rundown house, which had a sheet of plywood covering the downstairs window. "Kids will be kids, I suppose is what I'm saying. I certainly wouldn't condone what he did. I met my fair share of smart mouths in the army. We soon knocked the 'Big I am' attitude out of them, I can tell you. Oops, I shouldn't have told you that."

Sally sniggered. "I always thought you were a bit of a thug."

Jack opened his mouth to object, and Sally punched him in the leg. "Come on; we'll leave this discussion for another time. Let's see what we make of Raymond Lord for now."

"By the looks of this place, maybe we should go in there wearing rubber gloves," Jack grumbled as they walked up the cracked concrete path, dodging the stinging nettles off to their left that dominated the front garden.

"I take it Lord lacks any gardening talent. A bit like you in that respect," Sally teased.

"Cheeky mare. I'll have you know I have many talents in that department, although they do tend to focus on the massive gas barbecue we treated ourselves to at the end of last year."

"That figures. Right, straight faces now." Sally rang the doorbell, wiped her hand on her black suit trousers, and pulled a disgusted face at her partner.

The door was eventually opened by a tall, skinny man in his late fifties or early sixties. He squinted against the daylight. "Yeah?"

"Mr. Lord?"

"That's right, and you are?" The door closed a little as if he intended to slam it in their faces if he didn't care for their response.

Sally and Jack showed the man their IDs while Jack snuck his foot into the gap just in case. "DI Sally Parker and DS Jack Blackman of the Norfolk Constabulary. Is it possible for us to speak to you privately for a moment, sir?" Sally asked.

"About what?" he asked menacingly, inching the door their way again.

"Concerning your daughter, Gemma."

The door opened again, and the man stood back to let them in. "The place is a tip."

"That's okay. We're not here to judge your domestic skills."

"Good job, 'cause I haven't got any. This way."

He showed them upstairs to a second-floor flat that looked as though it hadn't been touched by either a duster or vacuum in months. Sally's nostrils flared as they filled with the smell emanating from the pile of takeaway cartons in the corner of the room and a more recent one, floating with grease, sitting on the coffee table in front of the sofa.

"Take a seat, if you want to risk it."

"We'll stand if it's all the same to you."

Lord shrugged and flopped into the sofa. A cloud of dust burst from the cushions and surrounded him like a mist. He coughed and waved the dust away from his face.

Shit! The quicker we get out of this shithole, the better.

"So, what's my darling daughter been up to then? She's not the type to get in trouble with you lot."

Sally exhaled a large breath. "It is with regret that I have to tell you that your daughter died in the early hours of this morning."

Lord bolted upright on the sofa. "What? Is this some kind of joke?"

"No. I'm very serious about this, Mr. Lord. I also have to tell you that your daughter's death is being treated as a murder enquiry."

He reached for a can of lager sitting on the table and downed the contents before he spoke. "Who did it?"

"It's our intention to find that out, Mr. Lord. Do you have any suggestions?"

"What the fuck? Why would I have a clue about that?"

He stared long and hard at Sally, and she responded with a challenging stare of her own. "Maybe you have an inclination. When was the last time you saw your daughter?"

"I don't know."

Sally noted that he was avoiding eye contact with her after his initial glaring session. "Try to think. It could be vital to the investigation, Mr. Lord."

He looked up. "Why? What are you insinuating? That I killed her? You are, aren't you?" He ran an agitated hand through his thinning, steel-grey hair.

"No. We'll be questioning all family members and friends alike. It's what we do during an investigation. Now please, answer the question."

"I honestly can't remember. I suppose it was around four to five months ago."

"And you've not had any contact since? Via the phone, I mean."

"No."

"Can I ask why not?" Sally wanted to see if he would admit the real reason he'd fallen out with his daughter.

"Time flies when you're having fun," he replied sarcastically.

"It must do when you have a full-time job. What do you do for a living, Mr. Lord?"

His jaw moved from side to side as though her question made him grind his teeth for some reason.

"Why the hesitation, Mr. Lord?" Jack prompted. "Tell the inspector."

"Nothing. I've tried to find a job, but no one will employ me."

"So you spend your days here?" Sally asked.

"Yeah, is that a crime?" he bit back.

"No, of course not. In that case, you really don't have an excuse why this place shouldn't be kept tidy, do you?" Sally asked, surveying the filthy lounge.

"Fuck off! That's a woman's job, not a man's."

Jack took a step forward and bent down to look the offensive man in the eye. "Show the inspector some respect, all right?"

"Whatever. Tell her to stop issuing dumb statements then."

Jack stepped back to stand beside Sally. "I apologise. I shouldn't have questioned your abilities in that department. Are you married, Mr. Lord?"

"There you go again, asking dumb questions. Do you think this place would look like this if I was married?"

"I doubt it. We were informed that you had remarried."

He opened another can of lager and took a long swig. "I bet I know who told you that, too. That bitch of an ex-wife of mine. Am I right?"

"We have had a conversation with your ex-wife this morning. However, it was your son-in-law who told us about an incident which occurred the last time you visited his home."

His chin hit his chest. "I regretted that as soon as it happened. I should never have hit the child."

"Then why did you?"

"I snapped. Gemma didn't leave me much option to say no to baby-sitting the child. Children and their care ain't a forte of mine. When I came home to tell Gina, the wife, she went ballistic. We rowed for days. In the end, I told her to fuck off out of my life. I never thought she would take me up on the bloody suggestion. Now, every time I try to contact her, she hangs up. Look at this place—she should be here, clearing up after me. It's her job."

"Really? You make the mess and expect other people to go out of their way to clear up after you?"

"Oh, fuck off, bitch. Get off your high horse and cut the crap about women having rights. A woman's place is in the home, looking after her man."

Sally felt the colour rise in her cheeks. She could see the man had an arrogant streak running through him not dissimilar to her ex-husband's. She was glad to see that Gina Lord had the sense to stand up to the pitiful excuse for a human being before he'd caused her irreparable damage. "You keep telling yourself that, Mr. Lord. While you're doing that, look around you at your home and ask yourself if it degenerated into resembling a pigsty before or after your wife left you."

He flung an arm in the air, batting away her suggestion. "Whatever!"

"Okay, now that you've opened the floodgates as to how you regard women, I need to ask if your daughter has contacted you this week."

He folded his arms and glared at Sally. "No, I've already told you that."

"Then I need to ask if your daughter ever confided in you if someone was treating her poorly."

"Treating her poorly? What's that supposed to mean? Do you think one of the family did this? Is that what you're getting at?"

"We don't know yet. It's been suggested to us that might be a genuine possibility. I need to ask if you have any witnesses as to your whereabouts last night."

He launched himself off the chair and stormed toward Sally.

Jack stood between them and forced Lord to retreat. "Back off, buddy. Just answer the question without the aggressive stance, okay?"

Lord paced the room. "And what if I don't have a witness or alibi for last night? Huh? What happens then?"

Sally shrugged. "Then we will ask your neighbours if they heard or saw you in the house, and if nothing comes from that, then we'll take you in for questioning."

"As a suspect? Are you effing mad? This is my daughter we're talking about here, not some low-life prostitute."

"Your estranged daughter, Mr. Lord. I'm baffled by your reference to her being a prostitute, unless you're trying to tell us something."

"That's it! Twist my effing words inside out and upside down. That'll make a change, won't it?"

"I'm doing nothing of the sort. You raised the subject. I'm just following up on what you said."

He threw himself onto the sofa again. "If I get my hands on the animal who did this…"

Sally could see the man was genuinely upset. Feeling a sudden pang of guilt, she tempered her off-handedness towards him. "Hopefully, we'll find the person before you do. I need to ask you again if Gemma ever hinted at someone showing her any kind of affection that they shouldn't have."

"In the family?"

"Not necessarily. Anyone at all?"

Lord shook his head in defeat. "No, not that I know of, but then, I don't suppose she'd ever confide that sort of information in me. Did you ask her mother the same question?"

"I did. She gave us a list of possible suspects to question."

"Shit! I'm assuming that my name was at the top of that bloody list. Oh, don't bother answering. Why else would you be here? It's written all over your face that you think I've got something to hide."

"I'm sorry if that's how it's coming across, Mr. Lord. All I'm doing is trying to ascertain if someone was carrying a grudge against your daughter and could have hated her enough to want to kill her. I'm sure you can understand that, yes?"

He nodded reluctantly and exhaled noisily. "I get that. But I repeat, I didn't do it. I might not have shown her when she was alive, but believe me, in my own way, I loved my daughter and would never intentionally harm her."

"Physically anyway, eh?" Sally corrected him after recalling how badly he'd treated Gemma over the years.

Lord glared at her for an instant then broke eye contact and nodded again. "I suppose you're entitled to your opinion. I'll admit to not being the best father in the world, but at least she understood me, unlike others I could mention. She knew I would always be there if ever she truly needed my help."

"Like taking care of her daughter when she left you in charge of the infant, you mean?" Sally issued him an assassin-type smile attached to the allegation, to keep him on his toes, just in case he thought he was steering her in the direction of crossing him off her list of suspects. Sally had no intention of doing such a thing until a full background check had been carried out and she'd spoken to anyone connected with the victim.

Lord remained silent and crossed his arms.

"Okay, I think we're done here, for now, at least. Please don't think about leaving the area, Mr. Lord. I'd hate to issue a warrant for your arrest."

"Can you do that? Force me to stick around here?"

"Try me," Sally stated triumphantly and turned on her heel towards the front door with Jack hot on her tail.

"Where to now, boss?" Jack asked, slamming the door.

Sally narrowed her eyes, contemplating their next move. "I'm dying to question Mark's brother, Colin, but something is telling me not to jump in too quickly on that front. So let's get back to the station and see what we can dig up about the brother before we go and tackle him."

"Makes sense," Jack agreed and hopped in the passenger seat of the car.

CHAPTER FIVE

The second Sally and Jack stepped back into the incident room, she gathered the team to go over what they had learned so far. Standing at the whiteboard, Sally picked up the marker pen and noted down the names of interest and their relationship to the deceased.

"So far, we've tentatively questioned the husband, Mark. We'll need to revisit him to question him further once he's got used to the idea of his wife not being around. I'm not sure what to think about him, or his mother, just yet."

"How did things go with the father, boss? Did the background check I sent over prove to be of any use?" Joanna asked.

"It did, Joanna. Apparently, his second wife has now thrown in the towel and deserted him."

"You should have seen the state of his house. We thought about calling in the fumigators before we questioned him," Jack added with a shudder.

Sally laughed. "He isn't joking when he says that, either. The place was a dump. Again, in spite of his previous convictions, the jury is still out on that one for me, too. Which at the moment, leaves us with one other family member to interview and Gemma's friends. I want to do a thorough check on Colin Whiting first before we pay him a visit. Maybe Jack and I should see Colin while someone else tracks down the friends and questions them. Any volunteers?"

Jordan and Stuart both raised their hands. Sally paused for a moment then looked at Joanna. "I'd really like Joanna to go, and maybe one of you guys could accompany her. Sort it out amongst yourselves, eh?"

Joanna nodded. "Fine by me. Which of you lovely gentlemen wants to be my chauffeur for the day?" She chuckled as the two men shook their heads.

"All right, I'll do it," Jordan volunteered after a moment or two.

"Thanks. Right, that's sorted. Before you head off, I want us all to see what we can find out about the suspects we have so far. Anything and everything, even down to where they shop for their underwear—got that?"

"What about TV and press coverage, boss? Do you want me to organise that before heading off?" Joanna asked, ever the practical member of the team.

"I'd like to leave that for twenty-four hours this time. Let's see what the pathologist has to report regarding the post-mortem first."

Sally left Jack to supervise the team as each of them hit their computers for the next few hours while she sifted through her post and attended to the paperwork cluttering her desk. Thankfully, she'd been fortunate to stay on top of it for the past month. Sally rejoined the team midway through the afternoon, her tummy grumbling because she'd bypassed yet another lunch hour. "Right, what do we have?"

Jack approached the whiteboard as the team shuffled into position with their notebooks to hand. "First up is Colin Whiting. I went through any files we had on him and came up with a sexual assault charge."

"Really? That's interesting." Sally filled the rest of the team in on what Gemma's mother had divulged about Mark's brother. "I got the impression that she felt Colin was intimidating Gemma. If he's got that kind of rap sheet, then she could be onto something. Do we know any more details about that case, Jack?"

He wrote the information on the board with the marker pen as he spoke. "It was a few years back. He'd worked shifts alongside the victim for a few months at the bakery."

"Ugh… I take it we're talking about the graveyard shift. All kinds of freaks appear around that time of night," Sally stated. "What was the outcome?"

"He lost his job, and the girl refused to drop the charges. He pleaded guilty and got an eighteen-month sentence."

"I suppose that's better than nothing. Hardly a deterrent, though, right?"

"Yep, my thoughts exactly."

"Marital status, Jack?"

"He's married a girl since the incident. Not sure if he knew her before or not. I'm assuming he didn't."

"Interesting. We'll tread carefully there when we question him."

"Does he work now?"

"Yes, he found a job as a baker in a small family-run bakery in Keswick."

Sally looked up at the clock on the wall—it was coming up to four o'clock. "Maybe we should shoot over there now, see if we can catch him at home before he starts his shift, if he's working tonight."

"Sounds like a plan. Want me to add the other info I've managed to find or leave that until later?"

"Depends if you've found out anything significant, Jack."

"Not really. I'm taking an authoritative call and saying the rest of this can wait. Questioning this bastard should be our priority."

Sally nodded at her partner's enthusiasm. "Then I'm happy to go along with that. Joanna and Jordan, why don't you set off now, too? Let's all meet back here at six this evening to discuss our findings."

Everyone agreed and departed, leaving Stuart to man the phones.

"Okay, here we are. Let's go in nice and calmly. Give him the benefit of the doubt from the start and go from there."

"I'll take my cue from you, as always, boss. Two cars in the drive; looks like his wife is at home, too."

"Maybe. We'll soon find out." Sally locked the car and joined her partner around the passenger side of the car. Together, they walked up the gravel driveway to the semi-detached house, which had a rounded bay window.

The door was opened by a tall, slim man in his early thirties. "Yes?"

Sally flashed her warrant card and introduced herself and her partner. "We'd like a quick chat with you, if you don't mind?"

"Concerning what, Inspector?" Colin Whiting asked, his eyebrows knitting together.

"About your sister-in-law, Gemma," Sally replied, deliberately being evasive, trying to gauge his reaction.

Colin took a step forward, pulled the door closed behind him, and leaned in to whisper, "I don't understand. What's Gemma been saying about me?" He gazed nervously over his shoulder several times.

Sally had seen enough to know that this man had a few secrets where his sister-in-law was concerned, and she intended to uncover those secrets. She leaned in and whispered back at him, "Let us in, and you'll find out. Either that, or we can carry out our interview down at the station."

He shuffled his feet and closed his eyes. Opening them again, he shrugged. "You better come in. My wife's at home, though."

"That's okay. We'll need to question her too."

"You're not making any sense."

Sally disarmed the man with a smile. "All will be revealed once we're inside, Mr. Whiting."

He led them through to a spacious, bright living room. A woman was sitting on a leather sofa in the bay window, stroking a puppy. Sally smiled at the woman and flashed her ID again. "I'm Detective Inspector Sally Parker, and this is my partner, DS Jack Blackman, of the Norfolk Constabulary. I take it you're Mrs. Whiting?"

"Yes. I'm Leona." She glanced at her husband waiting by the door. "Colin, what's this about?"

"Why don't we all take a seat, and we'll fill you in. Cute dog. What is it?"

"She's a shih tzu. Only eight weeks old. Sleeps a lot and poos even more." Leona laughed.

Sally sat on the other sofa, alongside Jack, and looked up expectantly at Colin, waiting for him to join his wife before she began talking.

Colin took the hint and sat close to his wife and the dog, which stirred for a mere second then went back to sleep. "I'm glad you're both at home. Can I ask if any members of your family have contacted you today, Colin?"

He frowned and nervously glanced sideways at his wife. Leona tapped his leg with the palm of her hand. "Answer the inspector, love."

"Sorry, no. No one has rung me. They know better than to do that when I've worked a shift the night before. Why?"

"Okay, then unfortunately, I have some bad news for you." Sally deliberately paused for a few seconds, waiting for Colin to react in some way, but all she saw was the man wince when Leona's hand tightened around his thigh. "This morning, Gemma Whiting's body was found not far from her home."

Colin's eyes widened, and his mouth dropped open while Leona gasped and covered her own gaping mouth with her hand. "What? Was she involved in an accident?" Colin asked, finally recovering his voice.

"No. We're treating her death as suspicious... murder. Due to the injuries she sustained."

"Murder?" Colin stood up and walked over to the bay window. Glancing out, he added, "I can't believe it."

"It's true, I'm afraid. Were you close?"

He turned to look Sally in the eye and curled his lip. "She was my sister-in-law, for fuck's sake. Of course we were close."

"You might want to control that tongue of yours. There's no need to swear at the inspector," Jack warned.

Colin mumbled an apology then turned back to gaze out the window again. Jack shrugged at Sally, unsure whether to force the man to take a seat and listen or not.

"Please, take a seat, Mr. Whiting. There are a few questions I'd like to ask you," Sally ordered.

Colin glanced sharply over his shoulder. "*Me*? Why do you want to ask *me* questions?"

"It's what we do during an investigation, Mr. Whiting—question people. Please take a seat. I don't particularly like talking to a person's back."

He huffed out an impatient breath and reclaimed his seat next to his wife. Sally watched the reaction between the husband and wife for a moment as Mrs. Whiting stroked the back of her husband's hand, only for him to pull it out of her reach.

"Perhaps you can tell me if Gemma ever confided in either of you?"

"Confided? About what?" Leona asked, her fingers twisting the fabric of her trousers on her thigh.

"Perhaps she intimated that she feared someone. Did she ever say that she felt her life was in danger at all?"

Colin frowned. "No. Is that what you think? That someone has been stalking her?"

"We're merely trying to build a picture, Colin. So far, your brother and Gemma's mother have given us a few leads to chase up."

Colin's hand touched the right side of his face, then he coughed to clear his throat. "Maybe you could make us all a coffee, darling?" he asked his wife.

She scowled at him, but when she looked at Sally, her scowl quickly vanished. "Excuse my manners, Inspector. My husband's right; I should've offered you a drink. Tea or coffee?"

"We'll both have a coffee. Milk with one sugar, thank you," Sally replied, looking at Jack for his approval. He nodded his acceptance.

Leona left the room and closed the living room door behind her. Sally winked at Jack and said to Colin, "Is there a reason you just asked your wife to leave the room, Mr. Whiting?"

His cheeks reddened, and his shaking hand scratched the side of his face before he buried his head in his hands. Sally and Jack glanced at each other, and she gave him a knowing nod. Sally changed seats and sat on the sofa beside Colin. "What is it, Colin? You can tell us," she urged softly.

His head hung low, and he shook it. "I can't believe she's dead."

"Yes, it's a tragedy. When was the last time you saw Gemma?"

"A few weeks ago."

"At the family barbecue?" Sally enquired.

His eyes narrowed when he looked her way, and his hands clenched together. "It might have been."

"Either it was, or it wasn't, Colin. Which is it?"

"Yes," he mumbled.

"Right, do you want to tell me what went on that day?"

"Mark and Gemma invited everyone to their place for a family barbecue. We had the usual burgers and hotdogs and a few chicken wings. I can't remember what drinks were on offer. I stuck to cans of lager, if that helps."

The glint that had appeared in his eye unnerved Sally. *He's toying with me. I'll let him play for a second or two, if that's what he wants.* Sally smiled. "Sounds like fun. I love a good barbecue myself, especially in the height of summer. Don't you, Jack?"

"Can't beat it, boss. Nothing like a good old family barbecue to while away a Sunday afternoon. Not keen on me doing all the work, though. That's the only downside to barbecues in my house."

"Oh, I thought men were usually in their element, tossing bangers around and setting fire to the burgers. How about you, Colin?"

He shrugged and replied, "I don't go in for all that cooking lark myself, with or without a barbecue to hand."

Sally inclined her head. "But you're a baker, aren't you?"

"Precisely. I cook for a living. I don't intend partaking in it during my leisure time, as well."

"I see. I suppose I can appreciate your line of thinking there. I always thought men reacted differently when cooking on a barbecue. Maybe you're the exception…"

"Is there a point you're trying to make with all this drivel, Inspector?" he asked, expelling an impatient breath.

"Well, what I'm leading up to is this: a little birdie told us this morning that at this very barbecue, you were seen having some kind of confrontation with the deceased. Would you care to enlighten us about that?"

He wrung his hands. "It was a simple misunderstanding; that's all."

"About what?" Sally asked.

"Something that happened between us."

"I'm listening, Colin. We need to know what this is in reference to."

"Why? So you can add me to your list of suspects? I'm innocent, I tell you."

"Prove it. Tell me what the confrontation was about that day?" Sally probed.

He fell silent when Leona returned with a tray of drinks. "Is everything okay?" she asked, her eyes firmly set on her husband's dubious posture when she placed his mug of coffee in front of him on the table.

"Fine. Everything is just dandy. Are there any biscuits in the house, Leona?"

His wife tutted, and after placing the tray of drinks on the table, she wafted out of the room again.

"I'd rather not discuss this in front of her, if you don't mind."

"Why? Do you have something to hide? An extramarital relationship perhaps?"

"No," he snapped. "I'd just rather mine and Gemma's relationship remained private."

"Ah, but I'd rather it was out in the open, Colin. If you had a relationship with the victim that we should be aware of, then you need to be honest with us. Of course, if you'd rather we interviewed you down at the station, that's fine by me."

"Jesus, you're like a bloody Rottweiler with a bone."

"That's true. The sooner you realise that, the better. Now what is it to be?" Sally glanced at the door when she heard Mrs. Whiting's footsteps in the hallway.

"I'll come down the station. If Leona found out about this, she would take a knife to my knackers."

"Nice phraseology, Mr. Whiting. Shall we make arrangements for you to pay a visit to the station tomorrow then?"

"No, it'll have to be sometime next week."

Sally shook her head. "It's either tomorrow or here and now. I have a murder investigation to conduct, with a murderer out there on the loose. I'd call that an urgent matter, wouldn't you?"

Leona entered the room again, holding a plate of biscuits.

As Sally stood up with the intention of returning to her original seat to make room for Leona, Colin whispered, "Four o'clock, tomorrow."

Once seated again, Sally nodded at Colin, accepting the time he'd suggested, and continued asking general questions about the family. "Maybe you can tell us what Gemma and Mark's relationship was like?"

Leona picked up her mug and settled it between her hands. "They have their ups and downs, like we all do, I suppose. That's right, love, isn't it?" she asked her husband.

"More downs than ups in their case, I suspect, Leona—unlike us, of course."

Sally wondered if he was trying to deliberately cast aspersions in his brother's direction. "Thanks, we'll note that down. When you say more downs than ups, are you telling me that in your eyes their marriage was in trouble?"

Leona gasped. "No. I wouldn't put it as clear-cut as that, Inspector."

"What about you, Colin? I'd love to hear your perceptions of your brother's marriage. Care to divulge what you feel about it?" Sally asked, smiling.

"They love each other. Mark would do anything to ensure Gemma was happy. Yes, they had the odd spat, but I never once felt their marriage was problematic. What did Gemma's mum say about it?"

"That's between me and her. I don't usually pass personal information around like that, sorry. That's why we insist on questioning as many people as we can in cases such as this. If nothing else, it helps us to form a picture, sometimes a multi-faceted picture, of events leading up to a victim's demise."

"I understand that, Inspector, but surely no one in this family would ever dream of hurting Gemma. She is... I mean she *was* such a kind person and loved by a lot of people." Leona took a sip from her mug.

"That's often the case, Leona. It seems most of the cases that cross my desk are accredited to people of a nice disposition. I'd say it comes out at a seventy-five to a twenty-five percent ratio."

"Really? That does surprise me. Can you tell us how Gemma was killed? Sorry, if you've already discussed it while I was out of the room."

The woman's obvious question heightened Sally's suspicions towards Colin. Why hadn't he asked the same question in his wife's absence? Sally's focus remained on Colin when she answered his wife, "I'd rather not go into specific details right now, as the cause of death is yet to be determined by the pathologist, who is performing the post-mortem today."

"I see. Does she have to have one of those?" Leona shuddered, almost spilling the contents of her mug in the process.

"It's procedure. A post-mortem is a vital part of the puzzle in building a case against an assailant. You'd be surprised the clues we can pick up from examining a corpse. Most pathologists call the victims 'silent witnesses' for that very reason. We should know more by tomorrow—that's when our investigation will truly begin. For now, we'll go about making general enquiries, asking friends and relatives of the deceased if they know of any recent arguments or falling-outs the victim might have had with anyone."

Leona looked thoughtful for a moment or two. "I see. I can't really tell you if Gemma had fallen out with anyone lately. I wasn't that close to her, not like Colin. I suppose working odd shifts gave Colin the chance to pop over there for a chat, more than I managed anyway."

Colin stared at his wife aghast. "Hardly, love."

"Oh, come on. Lately I know you've been working a lot of overtime, but you used to pop over there quite often. He loves playing with Samantha, you see. We haven't been blessed with children of our own." She held her mug with one hand and reached out her other hand to touch her husband's. "We're going through fertility treatment now."

Colin's eyes rolled up to the ceiling. "Yes, love. That's in its infancy, Inspector. We have a long way to go before they enrol us on the scheme. Plus, there's the matter of trying to find the money to fund all the treatment, of course. Five grand is a lot of dosh for an ordinary couple like us to stumble across."

"I understand. Have you been trying for a baby long?"

Leona's eyes moistened. "About three years now. They're not sure what the problem is, but Colin working different shifts to me could be the cause of it. At least that's what the doctor seems to be suggesting."

Colin patted his wife's knee. "All right, love. Stop talking about it. You know how upset you get when you think about the subject."

Leona sniffled. "You're right. I'm sure we'll get our own little one soon enough."

Sally studied Colin. The caring way he patted his wife's knee was a vast comparison to the way he'd been moments earlier when he was alone with her and Jack. The man was a real Jekyll-and-Hyde character if ever she saw one.

"I hope that works out for you both soon, Leona. Okay, I think we have enough to be going on with for now. Mr. Whiting, would you mind showing us out?"

Colin walked ahead of Sally and Jack and opened the front door. He looked over his shoulder before he spoke, "I'll drop by the station tomorrow then."

"Four o'clock. I'll be in reception, awaiting your arrival with anticipation, Colin. Can't wait to hear what secrets you have to unveil."

He shrugged. "It's nothing major, I can assure you. But then, if it gets me off your hit list of suspects, then it'll be worth the inconvenience of coming to the station."

"I'll see you at four tomorrow. Look after your wife, Colin. I think she's suffering more than she is letting on about her infertility, by the looks of things."

"Don't worry, Inspector. I'm well aware of how fragile my wife is." With that, he shut the door, putting an end to the conversation.

"Little shit!" Jack mumbled.

They hopped in the car and headed back to the station. "What was your impression of him, Jack?"

"If you must know, it was mixed."

"Care to clarify that?"

"Well, one minute, I would have loved to bop him one on the nose, but then right at the end, when the couple were discussing their infertility, I felt like throwing a consoling arm around each of them. That must be hard, mustn't it?"

"Wanting a baby so much that you go down the fertility route?"

"Yeah. What a comparison to Teresa, eh? Apparently, she got pregnant the first time she had sex. What are the odds of that happening?" he complained.

"Quite high, actually, if I recall a magazine article I read last year about the subject. Not that it was of any interest to me of course." Sally wrinkled her nose. "I've never seen the attraction to cleaning up after a baby twenty-four-seven."

Jack laughed. "You wouldn't object to doing that to a puppy, of course, would you now?"

Her eyes left the traffic for a second as she turned to wink at him. "You know me so well. They don't bawl their eyes out, either."

"True enough. Hey, what do you think his big secret is?"

"I have no idea. I'm leaning towards him announcing that he and Gemma had some sort of affair or secretive friendship going on, that neither of them wanted to disclose to the rest of the family. Roll on tomorrow, if only to discount him from our enquiries. Shifty bugger all the same."

"There's something about him that didn't sit well with me. That's for sure," Jack said, nodding.

"Let's hope the others have found out more from Gemma's friends about what went on last night than we have."

"Me, too. Because as it stands, we've got very little to go on so far," Jack agreed.

CHAPTER SIX

There was a buzz in the incident room atmosphere when Sally and Jack returned.

"What's going on, Joanna?" Sally asked, perching her backside on the desk nearest the detective constable.

"Well, we questioned a few of Gemma's friends—not all, as one of them is away with her work. Anyway, it would appear that Gemma acquired a new admirer at the pub last night."

Sally raised an inquisitive eyebrow and leaned forward. "Tell me more. As in someone was pestering her?"

"That's not how it was coming across to me, boss."

"Hmm... that's going to certainly be worth chasing up, all the same. How many of the women did you get around to questioning, Joanna?"

"Only two out of the three, boss. One lady in particular was keen to help."

"Okay, make it a priority to track down the last one tomorrow. What's the name of the lady who gave you the information? What did she say exactly?"

Sally glanced up at the clock on the wall, aware that she was asking her team to work overtime. However, none of her colleagues appeared to notice the time and went about their duties while Joanna filled her in. "Miss Audrey James said that a man was standing at the bar, eyeing up Gemma. She said she felt Gemma made up an excuse about the pub being stuffy and that she needed to get some fresh air and went outside for a while. She noticed the man leave the bar and follow her friend out of the pub."

"I see. I don't suppose she was that intrigued to find out what they got up to outside. The body language between the two, if they met up, that is?"

"No. She was distraught when she found out about Gemma, full of self-recriminations. She said the conversation was far too interesting amongst the group, and she didn't even think to go after Gemma to see if she was okay."

"How long was Gemma missing? Could she tell you that?" Sally asked, disappointed.

"She guessed it was around ten minutes."

"Okay, what was the name of the pub again? I'll give them a call, see if they've got any CCTV cameras."

"The Red Lion at Cringleford."

"Okay, that's close to my parents' home. I could drop by instead on my way over there this evening," Sally replied, sitting upright and rubbing at her chin.

"Other than that, neither of the friends could really tell us much. They were both shocked by the news of Gemma's death. I left a card and asked them to contact us if they think of anything else concerning last night's events, or if they can recall any strange incidents that have taken place in Gemma's life recently, that she confided in them."

"Great job." Sally clapped her hands to gain the team's attention. "Okay, we've all done really well today. Let's go home, get some rest, and start afresh in the morning at eight. All right, everyone?"

The team switched off their computers. Sally watched her colleagues file out of the incident room then dipped into her office to make a call.

"Hi, Mum. Is it okay if I visit this evening?"

"You know it is, sweetheart. You must've known we'd have plenty of dinner spare this evening. How does lasagne and salad sound?"

"Perfect. Just shove mine in the microwave, Mum. I've got a quick call to make en route. I should be with you around seven to seven thirty."

Her mother chuckled. "Impossible with a salad, but I get what you mean, dear. Drive carefully, love."

Sally hung up and smiled at Jack, who was leaning against the doorframe. "She still thinks I'm a bloody child. Last words she said were 'Drive carefully'."

"I guess all mothers are the same, especially when they're related to coppers."

"I suppose so. What are you still doing here? I thought you would've left with the others by now."

Jack shrugged. "Thought I could tag along to the pub with you."

Sally frowned. "I'm not going there to sample their finest liquid refreshments, Jack. It's work related. It'll be a straight in-and-out job."

"That's all right. I can still tag along, can't I? I'll follow you in my car. After we've obtained the info, we can go our separate ways."

She tilted her head and narrowed her eyes. "What's this really about? I'm guessing one of two things are riffling through that complex brain of yours."

He opened his mouth, ready to object, but she raised a hand to silence him.

"Either you're looking for an excuse not to go home, or—and this is the more likely reason springing to my mind right now—you're trying to protect me, the way you always do when we deal with a female victim who has been attacked in mysterious circumstances."

He held an imaginary gun to his head and pulled the trigger. "Guilty as charged on the second count, boss. Just humour me, eh?"

"All right, this will be the last time, okay? I'm aware this is a side effect from living with an abusive moron like Darryl. However, he's out of my life and not liable to intrude on it again any time soon. Got that?"

"I know. This will be the last time, I swear."

"It better be," she grumbled, rising to her feet and following him out of the office.

When they arrived at the pub, at around six thirty, a few punters were at the bar and a couple of families were sitting outside in the children's play area, making the most of the warm evening sun. A bearded man in his forties was leaning against the bar, engrossed in a chat with some of the customers. When Sally and Jack entered the lounge bar, he approached them with a welcoming smile that showed off a few crooked and missing teeth.

"What can I get you, folks, on this fine autumnal evening? The food won't be available until seven, as the chef had to attend a family funeral today. Finest in the area, so well worth the wait, although I might be a little biased there." He laughed and winked.

Sally immediately warmed to his friendly nature and made a mental note to call back another time to sample the menu with her mother and father, maybe at the weekend. She produced her warrant card, and in a hushed voice, she asked, "Are you the manager or owner of this establishment?"

The man crossed his arms and nodded. "The owner. Bill Warburton. Something wrong, miss?"

"Can we talk in private? In an office perhaps?"

The man nodded. "Terence, watch the bar while I deal with these nice people, will you?"

The young man he'd spoken to was sitting on the other side of the bar. He hopped off his stool, lifted the bar flap, and stood behind the beer pumps.

"Sorry, didn't mean to cause you any inconvenience."

The owner waved her suggestion away. "You haven't. He was due to start work in half an hour anyway. I'll see him right with an extra pint after his shift." He showed them through to a whitewashed room, stacked full of pub supplies. "Excuse the mess. We had a delivery earlier, and I just shoved them in here, out of the way. What's this about, Inspector?"

The room was bare as far as seating options were concerned. "Well, we're investigating the murder of one of your customers."

"What? Who?" The man seemed shocked by the news and stumbled backwards against the wall behind him.

"A Gemma Whiting. Do you know her?"

He shook his head and frowned. "Don't recognise the name. A lot of folks pass through these doors, though, that I can't really put a name to. Do you have a picture?"

"Sorry, no. She was in here last night with a group of friends. Does that ring a bell?"

He clicked his fingers. "Audrey was in here last night with some friends. I haven't met them before, so I have no idea what their names are."

"Okay, here's the thing. Audrey told us that Gemma went outside during the course of the evening. It's possible that she might have met up with a man. Do you have any form of CCTV either inside the pub or surveying the exterior?"

"I do. Wow, I'll go and check the machine, see if it was working last night. Fingers crossed, eh?" He rushed out of the room, seeming eager to help, and returned a few minutes later. He gave them the thumbs-up. "Do you want to come through to the other office and take a look?"

"Incredible news. I really wasn't expecting that."

Sally and Jack followed the man into an even smaller office. They all squeezed into the confined space full of shelves, storing bulging boxes of what Sally presumed to be the pub's accounts.

"Excuse the mess. One of these days, I'll get around to clearing up this place. You know how it is."

"There's no need to apologise. Is it a CD you have or video?"

"It's a CD. I can make you a copy, if you like?"

"Let's see what we have first, Bill."

He ran the tape. Sally leaned in closer to the grainy picture. "Can we make it clearer at all?"

The man messed around with the contrast a little and came up trumps. The film consisted of Gemma Whiting, walking out of the pub's back door and into the children's play area at the rear.

"Well, she's alone so far," Jack pointed out.

Within seconds, a man appeared at the door of the pub, and without faltering in his stride, he marched over to where Gemma was sitting.

"If I didn't know any better, I would say that meeting was arranged. Look at her reaction—she's smiling at him. I'm not sure I'd treat his interruption with as much grace. In fact, I would be treating him warily," Sally said, shaking her head.

"Yeah, but then you're a copper, boss. You have a built-in scumbag radar."

She laughed at her partner's turn of phrase. "Except where exes are concerned, eh? I'll still take that as a compliment, Jack." She returned her attention to the couple on the screen. "They seem to be getting along pretty well, would you say?"

Both men observing the film with her nodded their agreement.

"Do you recognise the man at all, Bill?"

"I think I've seen him in here once or twice. Let me get a printout and ask Terence. He's lived in the area all his life. If anyone knows this guy, he will. I'll be right back." He ran the disc backwards and stopped the film at a spot where the man's face was as clear as possible, considering the footage had been taken during the night-time.

After Bill had printed off the picture and left the room, Sally set the disc in motion again, and together she and Jack continued to voice their suspicions.

"His mannerisms aren't really signifying any evil intent towards her, not to me anyway," Sally said.

"Hmm… I'm thinking along the same lines. Apart from startling her initially, the more I see of the film, the more it looks like just a couple of old friends having a chat. Is he pointing out that Porsche?"

Sally peered closer at the man's pointing finger. "It appears that way to me, Jack. We'll ask Bill if he knows who it belongs to."

The owner of the pub returned, beaming. "I've got a name for you, folks."

Sally stood up and cocked her head. "Really? That's fabulous news. Jack, get this down, will you?"

Her partner scrambled for his notebook and pen, poised for action.

"It's Taylor Hew. Now that I've heard the name, I do recognise him as being local. He's only stepped foot in the pub a few times, though. He lives within a ten-mile radius of here, according to Terence."

"That's excellent. I don't suppose you know what car he drives?"

Bill frowned. "No, I could ask Terence."

"In a moment." Sally rewound the disc to where the man motioned towards the vehicle they suspected belonged to him. "Here. It looks like they are discussing this car. It's a Porsche. Would he likely be driving one of those?"

"I'd have to ask Terence. Look, why don't I make a copy of the disc for you, and then I'll take over from Terence at the bar and let you have a chat with him?"

"Perfect. We really appreciate your assistance. It's important we catch the culprit who attacked Gemma quickly. If this man is innocent, it's just as important for us to discount him from our enquiries ASAP."

He nodded and set about his task. Sally and Jack left the room to give him the space he needed to work. "Want to drop by this bloke's house tonight?" Jack asked.

Sally winked at her partner. "If his place is near, we might as well."

"Thought you might say that," Jack grumbled good-naturedly.

"So glad I didn't disappoint you, Jack."

Bill walked out of the office, handed the CD case to Sally, and marched up the corridor back into the bar area. "Take a seat there, and I'll ask Terence to join you in a sec."

Sally and Jack waited another minute or two for the young man with spiky red hair to sit down opposite them.

"The boss tells me you want to have a quick chat about Taylor Hew."

"That's right. Do you know him well?" Sally asked.

Jack flipped open his notebook and began taking notes.

"I know *of* him. Couldn't really say that I know him well. What's he done?" he asked, grinning cheekily.

"We just want to have a chat with him. Do you know what car he drives?" Sally batted away the young man's question with one of her own.

"One of those posh sporty cars. Sorry, cars aren't really my thing."

"Do you think it might be a Porsche?" Jack prompted him. "Everyone knows what a Porsche looks like."

The man's eyes widened. "Er... not me, sorry. Not unless you tell me what colour it is. I'm good with colours. That's about all, though."

"The thing is, it's hard to make out the colour of the car on the CCV footage we've viewed. Never mind, we'll do a check on the database tomorrow and see what we come up with. Bill told us you thought the man was local."

"Sort of. He's not a regular here but pops in now and again. I can't give you his exact address, but I know it's around the Ketteringham area. I think I overheard him mention that he was looking at buying a property close to where he lives now, and Ketteringham came up in the conversation."

"That's great. I don't suppose you happen to know where he works."

"I think he's one of these up-and-coming property-developer types."

"Okay, that's a start at least. Is he married?"

The young man shrugged and shook his head. "That, I can't tell you."

"Never mind. You've been really helpful. We'll let you get back to work now." All three of them rose from their seats. Sally waved at the owner of the pub and mouthed goodbye to him.

Outside Jack asked, "Do you want me to get on to control for his address?"

Sally looked at her watch. "Why not? Mum's going to be pissed off with me being late anyway. What does another few minutes matter? Are you all right to continue?"

"Shit happens. This is important, boss. We need to chase it up ASAP."

"I'm glad you agree. You call the station, and I'll ring my mother." They stood at opposite ends of Sally's car and placed their calls. "Mum, it's me. Sorry, I'm going to be held up."

"That's all right, dear. I'll dish up ours and put yours aside for when you get here. Nothing major wrong, I hope?"

"It could be, Mum. I'll tell you all about it later. Thanks for understanding. Sorry for messing you around. See you later." Sally ended the call as Jack joined her.

"Okay, I have his address. Want to take the two cars again?"

"Makes sense, and then we can go our separate ways afterwards."

"I'll lead the way then," Jack suggested.

Sally waited for Jack to drive past her. She tailed him through the windy country lanes until they finally arrived at Taylor Hew's address. The gated house was spectacular; white with rounded windows sitting under an impressive reed-thatched roof. Jack joined her as she got out of her car. "Bloody hell. I think I'm in the wrong career."

"We both are, Jack. I can't see his car anywhere. Can you?"

"It could be in a garage. Hard to see what's on the other side of the wall from here. Let me try the intercom."

Sally got up close to the gate and strained her neck when she tried to look around the front wall, alongside the gates, of the impressive house. It proved to be a waste of time.

"No answer. Looks like your first assumption was accurate. Maybe he's out on the prowl for his next victim."

"You can cut that out, matey. We don't know he's guilty of anything other than talking to Gemma yet. Let's hold fire on casting such aspersions for now, okay?"

Jack shrugged. "Okay. What do you want to do now?"

"We should call it a day. Maybe get on to the station again, ask uniform to keep an eye out for the car. There can't be that many Porsches in the area. We can come back tomorrow to question Taylor Hew."

Sally got out of the car at her parents' home and paused when she heard the commotion coming from the kitchen. She slipped her key in the door and stood in the hallway, listening to her parents arguing. Dex ran up the hallway to greet her. She placed a finger to her mouth and told her faithful companion to be quiet. He rolled over and demanded a tummy tickle while she continued to listen to the confrontation her parents were having.

"Don't give me that same old excuse, Christopher. That bloody job has been half-completed for months now. I'm fed up with tripping over that damn pipework. You *promised* me you'd have it finished by the start of the summer, and now we're swiftly moving into the autumn."

"But, Janine, you know my circumstances. The paid work has to come first. Either that or the bank is liable to repossess the house."

"And whose bloody fault is that? I told you—no, I *begged* you—not to take out that blasted loan last year. I'm nearing sixty, for Christ's sake! The last thing I wanted was any kind of mortgage or loan around my neck at my age. I should never have listened to you in the first place."

Sally's eyes teared up. She had no idea her parents were riddled with debt. She knew her father had been ripped off by someone he'd carried out some building work for the previous year, but her parents had kept from her the fact that they were short of money. She wished she could help them out financially, but Darryl had left her high and dry in that respect. Hence the tiny flat in Norwich.

Dex's moaning increased. He was such a sensitive soul; hated the sound of raised voices. Sally decided that she'd heard enough and walked into the kitchen, where she found her parents on opposite sides of the room, glaring at each other.

Her mother's mouth dropped open the second she saw Sally. Recovering well, she said, "Hello, darling, not as late as you anticipated then, after all."

"Cut the crap, Mum. I heard you arguing. Why didn't you tell me things were so bad?"

Her father cleared his throat then threw himself into a chair at the table. "To be frank with you, love, it's none of your concern. You've had more than enough shit of your own to deal with this year. Why should we heap our burdens on your young shoulders, too?"

Sally walked over, placed a gentle arm around her mother's shoulder, and guided her to the table. After pushing her into the chair next to her father, Sally sat down opposite them and reached for each of their hands. Her father's was hot and sticky, which immediately caused her to worry about his heart. He'd had serious health issues over recent years and was still under the specialist. "Okay, you guys need to listen very carefully to what I have to say, without interruptions."

Both her parents nodded and took turns sighing heavily.

"We'll listen, although I have a feeling we're going to feel like chastised children at the end of our little chat," her mother said, her own eyes moist with tears.

"If you think that, Mum, then you really don't know me well."

Her mother opened her mouth to speak again, but Sally issued her a warning glance, and her mother reconsidered her actions.

"I'm disappointed that you have let things slip to this stage. You should have told me, even asked my advice. Whether you care to admit it or not, I'm a grown woman, not a child anymore. Yes, I've had my problems this year. However, that doesn't mean that I have to wallow in self-pity and ignore what is piling high on your plates at the moment. If you need financial help, then I'm going to give it to you. No arguments, you hear me? Don't answer that—it was a rhetorical question. Thanks to your kindness, I moved in a few months back when I was in trouble. If you'll have me back, I propose giving up my teeny-weeny flat and move in here. How about that? Will you have me?"

Tears flowed freely from her mother's eyes, and she grabbed her husband's hand. "Only if you're one hundred percent sure, darling."

"I agree, with one stipulation," her father stated.

Sally tilted her head. "What's that, Dad?"

"That your name goes on the deeds of the house."

Her mother glanced sharply his way then back at Sally. "What a great idea. That would work well for all of us."

"I was going to suggest that I should take over the mortgage payments. I'm doubtful about my name appearing on the deeds, though."

Her mother's beautiful smile returned, pushing aside the tension that had crumpled her forehead moments earlier. "It makes sense. Although, I do think we should contemplate going halves on the mortgage repayments. I'd hate to feel as though we were using you, love."

"No, Mum. It's all or nothing. I take it the house would be left to me in your wills anyway, so all we'll be doing is bringing the date forward, yes?"

Her father left his chair and circled the table. He pulled Sally to her feet and squeezed her in a suffocating hug. "I can't thank you enough for this, love. If it hadn't been for that bastard ripping me off last year, we wouldn't be in this mess. That'll teach me not to trust folk again."

"No good blaming yourself, Dad. Doing this will benefit all of us in the long run. I miss you guys and the little man over there." Sally looked over at Dex curled up on his bed, eyeing them all, wondering what was going on. "I'll make an appointment to see the bank manager as soon as I can, although I have another big case to contend with as of today. I'll tell you about it after dinner. Come on, Mum, shake a leg. I'm ravenous."

"Cheeky! It's all ready, love. It just needs zapping for a few minutes. Christopher, I know we don't usually drink during the week, but this is cause for a celebration. Break open that good bottle of wine we've been saving for a special occasion."

Sally's father didn't need telling twice. While Sally took the glasses from the glass cupboard in the kitchen, her father sought out and opened the nice bottle of Chateauneuf-du-Pape Sally herself had bought her parents a few years earlier.

What started out as a gloomy evening turned into a lovely family get-together full of happy memories. Bedtime loomed before Sally realised she hadn't told her parents about the case she was working on. After inviting herself to stay in the spare room, she decided to leave the conversation until the morning.

She sorted out a suitable change of clothes from the spare outfits she kept at the house then spent the night cuddled up to Dex. He moaned contentedly in her arms until they both fell asleep.

CHAPTER SEVEN

Sally left the house at seven thirty the next morning. The storm clouds that accompanied her to work did little to spoil her happy mood. Her heart was lighter after she'd seen the broad smiles plastered on her parents' faces, over the swift breakfast she'd consumed at her mother's insistence.

Jack's car was already in the car park when she arrived, so she made her way up to the incident room alone for a change. "Morning, Jack. Find a snake in your bed or something?"

"Ha, ha! I've been known to arrive before you on a few occasions. No need to make a big deal out of it."

"That'll be *very* few occasions. Any news on Taylor Hew from the night patrol?"

"Nothing. He didn't return home last night. Should we go out there this morning?"

"That's what I was thinking, unless something major crops up. Want a coffee?"

"Thanks."

Sally walked over to the vending machine and bought two coffees. She placed one on Jack's desk and took the other one through to her office to aid her in her attempt to tackle the morning post. About an hour into the chore, Sally's office phone rang. "Hello, DI Parker."

"Ma'am, we had an incident reported overnight that I think you should be aware of," the female voice on control informed her.

"What kind of incident? A murder?"

"No, ma'am. It does look like an attempted murder, though. The victim is in hospital."

"And you think this is related to the murder enquiry we're dealing with at the moment?"

"I think there are similarities, ma'am. Thought you should know right away."

"Okay, I'll look into it. Give me the details of the attack and the hospital the victim is in."

After jotting down the details of the incident, Sally hung up and shouted for Jack to join her.

He swiftly appeared in the doorway, wearing one of his notorious frowns. "You hollered, boss?"

"Get ready to go, Jack. I've just been informed about a brutal attack on a young woman. The attack took place down a country lane. Sound familiar?"

"Bloody hell. Are we talking about the same vicinity here?"

"Not far. I suppose ten miles away. The intriguing part is that it appears to be the same kind of attack. Anyway, we'll head out to the hospital and see for ourselves. Give me five minutes, okay?"

"Sure. Do you have the name of the victim? I'll do a quick search before we head off."

"Julie Smith. That'd be a help, thanks."

Sally quickly signed a few forms and put the sheets of paper in her out tray to deal with upon her return. Then she slipped on the jacket to her trouser suit and left the office. Jack followed her down to the car, filling her in on what information he'd managed to gather.

"Looks like she's single and lives not far from where the incident occurred, just like Gemma Whiting."

"Interesting. Especially after we found out that Taylor Hew didn't return home last night. Maybe we should put out an alert for him before we leave."

"Sticky ground for yanking him in."

"Yeah, I know. We could get uniform to keep an eye open for him and keep him under observation until we can get to him."

"Why uniform? Why not put either Jordan or Stuart on the task?"

By then, they had reached Sally's car. "Okay, you organise that for me, Jack, while I drive."

At the hospital, Sally showed the parking attendant her ID, and he told her to park at the rear. She and Jack rushed into the reception area and asked the receptionist what ward they could find Julie Smith in. It took a few minutes for the woman to find the patient in the system. Eventually, she told them that Julie had been placed in the Intensive Care Unit, and issued them with instructions on how to locate the ward. When they exited the lift, they found a doctor and nurse going through a patient's care at the desk outside the ICU ward.

"Hello, I'm DI Sally Parker, and this is DS Jack Blackman. We're here concerning the attack on Julie Smith. Can you tell us how she is?"

"I'm Dr. Carter. She's in a very sorry state, I'm afraid. Fractured skull and cheek. Broken arm, and we believe there is some internal bleeding."

"Ouch! I don't suppose she's conscious, is she?"

"No, and she's not likely to be for a few days at least, taking into consideration the injuries she's suffered."

"How awful. What are the chances of her pulling through, Doc?"

"Speaking realistically, I'd say about sixty percent, Inspector. It's the fractured skull I'm more concerned about right now. If a bleed appears, then that could be very dangerous indeed. She's under regular surveillance, and her vital signs are being monitored every thirty minutes without fail."

"So there's no point in us hanging around, hoping she'll regain consciousness?"

"I wouldn't waste your time, Inspector. I'd be out there, looking for the culprit instead."

"Okay. Can I leave you my card? Any news whatsoever, good or bad, would you contact me immediately?"

The doctor took the card from Sally and gave it to the nurse. "Of course. I hope you find the vile person who did this, Inspector, and quickly."

"So do I, Doctor."

Outside, in the car park, Jack complained, "Well, that was a waste of a morning."

"All right, Jack, no need to state the obvious. Let's get back to the station, see if Stuart has got any news for us. I'm also going to chase up the pathologist. He should have carried out the post on Gemma by now. I'll need to inform him of the connection to this case, too."

Sally blew out a long breath when they arrived in the incident room, and the rest of the team looked at her expectantly. "She's unconscious and in a very bad way. Which only makes me more determined to catch the bastard responsible. No word from Stuart yet?"

Joanna shook her head. "No, boss. I took a call from the pathologist about twenty minutes ago. Can you call him back?"

"It was on my to-do list anyway. Thanks, Joanna. Jack, can you chase up a next-of-kin for Julie Smith for me? That should be our next job. I'll be back soon."

Sally removed her jacket, placed it on the back of her chair, took a few deep breaths, then dialled the pathology department. "Hello, Simon. It's DI Parker. You rang me?"

"I did. Sorry about the delay. I would've had the results back from the post-mortem sooner, but a major incident took place last night, and it slipped my mind."

"Never mind. What do you have?"

"One very interesting fact for you: Gemma Whiting was around four weeks pregnant."

Sally fell back in her chair. "Shit! Four weeks, you say? Would she have known about the pregnancy, do you think?"

"She might have suspected, but I doubt she knew for sure. Maybe you should be asking her husband that question, Inspector."

"Oh, I intend to, don't worry. Do me a favour and make sure you get DNA evidence from the foetus."

"It's done already."

"I don't think this case will be tied up with a pretty bow come the end of the investigation," Sally said.

"That sounds ominous."

"Anything else, Simon?"

"No, nothing of significance other than what we covered at the scene. If you're contacting the family, would you mind passing on that I've been in touch with the funeral home?"

"Of course. I'll let them know. I'm sure it'll be a relief for them to hear. Thanks for letting me know. Oh, by the way, I've just come back from the hospital. There's a young lady there in ICU who was attacked in similar circumstances. I just wanted you to be aware. There's every chance she might not make it, so she could possibly end up as one of your 'patients' anyway."

"That's a shame. If we have a monster in our midst attacking women on country roads at night, maybe it would be wise for you to warn the general public via the media," Simon suggested.

"Thanks, Simon. The matter is in hand."

"Glad to hear it. Speak soon."

Sally hung up just as Jack appeared in the doorway. "Everything all right, boss?"

"I think the case just got interesting. Gemma Whiting was pregnant. By the way her husband reacted, I don't think he knew. Do you?"

Jack inclined his head. "What are you getting at, boss?"

"I'm not sure just yet. It's all going round in my mind at the moment. Let's see what Colin Whiting has to say when he visits later. Something tells me he might have an inkling about the pregnancy."

"Whoa, you think the brother-in-law knows but not the husband? That whiffs of them having an affair then."

"Let's not jump to any wayward conclusions just yet. I need to get in touch with the media. Is Stuart back yet?"

"Nope. Want me to chase him up?" Jack walked into the office and placed a sheet of paper on the desk in front of her. "The next of kin details for Julie Smith you wanted."

"Thanks. The tasks are mounting up already, aren't they? Okay, get in touch with Stuart. Maybe try and find a few properties that are owned by Hew and see if we can track him down that way. Does he work from an office? I'm not sure property developers do that even. Try and track one down if you can."

"Yes, boss."

Jack left the office, and Sally immediately picked up the phone to call her contact at the TV station. "Hi, Georgia. It's DI Sally Parker. Any chance I can ask a favour?"

"Sure, Inspector. What do you need?"

"A slot on today's news would be good." Sally crossed her fingers tightly and waited for the woman's response.

"Let me take a look at today's schedule, see what I can do. What's the case?"

"There are two actually. One murder and one violent assault, which has left the victim in an unconscious state in hospital. That's why it's urgent to inform the public. It needn't be a conference."

"Okay, well, that alters things. I can send a reporter over this afternoon, or you could just give me the details, and I'll go from there. You know I'll treat each case sympathetically."

Sally nodded. "That's why I only tend to deal with you, Georgia." She gave the woman the details of both cases, emphasising the need to issue a warning to the other womenfolk in the immediate area about the dangers of going out at night alone.

"That's fantastic. I'll run it tonight on the evening news. What about the newspapers? Are you going down that route, too?"

"Yep, I'm just about to contact a journalist I know now. Thanks for your help, Georgia. I appreciate it." Sally hung up and flicked through the pages of the contacts notebook she kept tucked safely in her desk drawer and prodded her finger at the name Phil Edmunds.

She dialled his mobile and tapped her pen while she waited for him to answer the call.

"Yep."

"Phil? It's DI Sally Parker. Do you have a minute?"

"For you, darling, anytime."

"Still practicing your charm-school chat-up lines, I see." Sally laughed.

"I take it I've screwed up again. Seriously, what's up, Sally?"

"Keep trying. One of these days I might bow to your pressure and let you buy me dinner."

"Wow, really? Cool."

"Back to business. I've got two cases that I need you to treat as high priority. Can you do that for me?"

"Of course. Let me grab a pen, and I'll take down the details. I can probably get it in my column either today or tomorrow. Will that suit you?"

"That would be ace, Phil. You're a star." She ran through the details of both cases then ended the call with a satisfied smile.

"I take it that went well," Jack asked from the doorway.

"I love it when things slot into place as intended. If only that could be said about solving Gemma's murder and Julie's attack. We should go and see Julie's parents next. Any news of tracking down an office for Hew?"

"Not yet. As far as we know, he works from home. I chased up Stuart, no good there."

"What about a contact number for Hew?"

"I'll get on to Companies House, see what information I can get out of them."

"Okay. The media are running the story—or should I say stories—over the next few days. Prepare the team for that, will you?"

"On it now."

Jack left the office and returned a few minutes later, looking smug and waving a sheet of paper. "Got his phone number. Want me to give him a ring?"

Sally winked at him and held out her hand for the sheet. "I think this needs a woman's touch."

Jack left the room, chortling.

Sally cleared her throat and thrust back her shoulders, ready for action. Using the landline, she dialled Hew's number. "Hello, is that Taylor Hew?"

"It is, and you are?"

"Sally Parker. I was talking to a friend about going into property development, and someone overheard me in the pub, and they mentioned your name."

"I see. Yes, it's my line of business. I'm always happy to share my experience with folks. What is it you'd like to know?"

"Any chance we can meet over a coffee? My treat."

"Sure, I have some spare time around two this afternoon."

"Wonderful. I live near Attleborough. What about the coffee shop in the high street? I'll even stretch to a sticky bun."

Hew laughed. "Deal. I'll be there at two."

Sally punched the air as she hung up. "Jack, in here a minute."

"Yes, boss."

"I have a coffee appointment at two with Taylor Hew."

"Whoa, he agreed to meet you?" His eyes narrowed. "Did you tell him you're a copper?"

Sally placed a finger to her lips. "Oh gosh, I knew I should have mentioned something."

"Let's hope the chief doesn't find out about this."

Sally pushed back her chair. "He won't. Now that's sorted, we should head out to see Julie's next of kin, see what we can find out there before I meet up with Hew."

CHAPTER EIGHT

"You just caught me. I'm on my way to the hospital to see my daughter."

"We'll only take five minutes of your time, Mrs. Smith. We're truly sorry about what has happened to Julie. Can I ask where she was last night?"

The woman sat down on the black suede sofa, her hands visibly shaking in her lap as she chewed on her lip. "Julie went into town with her friend Roger. There's nothing going on between them; they're just friends. I rang him earlier to tell him that Julie is in hospital, and he's beside himself. I asked him why he'd left her. He told me that he'd run into an old friend and that Julie insisted he should leave her and go to a nightclub with his friend. I told him off for leaving her alone. I know I shouldn't have done that, but he should have stayed with Julie, not deserted her."

"We'll need to get a statement from Roger, Mrs. Smith. Would you mind giving us his full name and address?"

She crossed the room and picked up the address book sitting beside the telephone. Jack jotted down the friend's details, and Mrs. Smith returned to her seat.

"I don't suppose Roger mentioned if Julie had a conversation with someone else during the course of the evening? Or whether someone was watching her?" Sally asked.

"I did ask him if anything strange had happened, but he said no. They had a good time and parted quite early."

"Has Julie got a boyfriend?"

"No. Not since she dumped that German fella, Hans."

"Hans? Does he live nearby?"

"No. He was on a foreign-exchange scheme at her work. As soon as she found out he had a regular girlfriend back in Germany, she dumped him. He left England not long after, probably because of the shame." She ran a hand over her face. "Why would anyone hurt my sweet daughter? She goes out of her way to help people. Never falls out with friends and rarely says anything bad about anyone. She's a good girl; she doesn't deserve this. I'm sorry, I need to go now. I want to be there when she wakes up—*if* she wakes up," she added sadly.

"I understand. We'll have a word with Roger, see if he can shed any light on what went on last night. I hope Julie recovers soon."

"So do I, Inspector. She's all I've got since her father passed away last year. If I lose her…"

"Hopefully, it won't come to that. Just keep thinking positively, Mrs. Smith. Do you need a lift to the hospital?"

"No, I have a car. Just promise me you'll get the sick individual who did this. All we hear nowadays is the amount of unsolved crimes there are. Please don't let Julie be added to those statistics."

"We're doing our best. Don't give up on us, Mrs. Smith."

Sally and Jack left the house. "Is it worth chasing up the ex?" Jack asked as they climbed into the car.

"I wouldn't have thought so. I think we should drop by Roger's place, however, and ask him what went on last night."

Before Sally could start the engine, Jack's mobile rang. He glanced her way and frowned. "It's Donna."

"Well, answer it. Don't keep her waiting. You know she never disturbs you at work."

"Hello, love."

Sally saw Jack's eyes widen. "What is it?" she mouthed.

Her partner shook his head and ran a hand through his short, greying hair. "All right. Calm down. Is the ambulance on its way? Okay, I'll meet you at the hospital." He hung up, looking distraught. "It's Teresa. Donna thinks she's gone into labour."

"What? Crap, you better get over there." Sally pulled away from the kerb and drove back to the station.

"It's too soon, Sally. She's only eight months gone."

"It might be all right, love. Not that I know anything about this sort of thing, of course."

"A sixteen-year-old going into prem labour—I can't see there being a positive outcome to that."

The rest of the journey was conducted in silence. She dropped Jack off at his car. "Good luck, matey. Ring me later if you get the chance. Love to Donna and Teresa."

"Thanks, boss."

Sally locked the car then stood and watched her partner drive away, as the squeal of tyres accompanied his exit from the car park. "Please let both mother and child be okay," she murmured, then went up to her office, where she decided to write down a plan of action for the day. At the top of the list, she put Roger Wilson's name. She would get one of the other members of the team to track him down to get a statement. Time was marching on, and she needed to leave some time free so that she could make her rendezvous with Taylor Hew at two o'clock. She was aware that she would need to take a partner with her in case things kicked off there, too. Then she needed to return to the station at four for her arranged interview with Colin Whiting. With everything in place, in her mind at least, she walked into the incident room and relayed the plan of action to her team.

"Okay, listen up, folks. We'll be a man down this afternoon as Jack received an urgent call from his wife. No point asking what it was about—that's up to him to tell you, not me. Anyway, he's left me with a pile of jobs to get through, so I'm going to delegate some of them out to you guys, all right?"

The team nodded, each of them wearing a puzzled frown.

"Jordan, I'd like you to track down a Roger Wilson. He accompanied Julie Smith on her night out, but they separated earlier than expected. We need to get a statement from him ASAP. The priority needs to be if Roger saw anyone taking interest in Julie before they split up. Also, see if she had any admirers at work who we should be looking at."

"Yes, boss. Is it all right to tell him what state the victim is in?"

Sally nodded. "Within reason. Just tell him that at present, she's unconscious. I think he'll probably know that fact by now from her mum." Looking at Stuart, she said, "Stu, you'll be joining me this afternoon. I've set up a meeting with Taylor Hew under the pretence of picking his brains about property development."

"Wow, and he fell for that? I waited and waited outside his home but eventually returned to base empty-handed. Sorry to let you down, boss."

"You haven't let me down, Stu. There's more than one way to flush out a rat from its sewer. Of course, he might be innocent in all this, so we still need to tread carefully. I've also been in touch with the media. Both cases will be on the TV news tonight and in the local paper either today or tomorrow, depending on whether Phil can write up the story before the deadline. So we need to be ready for an influx of calls over the next twenty-four to forty-eight hours. Joanna, I'll leave you in charge of that. Can you also keep checking regularly with the hospital for me, to enquire about Julie? The sooner we can question her about the incident, the better. It might send the case off in a whole different direction." Joanna smiled and bobbed her head. "Right, the other major thing clogging up my agenda today is the arrival of Colin Whiting at four o'clock, if he shows up. He better. Otherwise, I'll yank his arse in here so quickly, he'll burn the rubber off the soles of his shoes."

Joanna chuckled while Jordan and Stuart let out full belly laughs.

Rarely did Sally say anything she wasn't prepared to follow through on. "Okay, let's get this show on the road. Ready, Stu?"

***

"Are you set?" Sally asked her temporary partner when they pulled into the parking space close to the arranged meeting place.

"Yep. There's a guy sitting outside, messing about with his mobile. Do you think that's him?"

"There's only one way to find out. Just be ready to pounce on him if he tries to do a runner, okay?"

"Sure thing, boss."

They exited the vehicle and casually walked over to the man. He took an age to look up at them, even though their frames cast a shadow over his phone as he was texting.

Sally coughed. "Mr. Hew?"

He completed his text and stabbed a button to send it on its way. "That's right. Miss Parker, I take it."

Sally flashed him a smile, along with her warrant card. "That'll be Detective Inspector Sally Parker of the Norfolk Constabulary. You're a hard man to track down, Mr. Hew. Mind if we take a seat? Oh, this is my partner, DC Stuart McBain."

He shrugged, no significant expression showing on his face. "Be my guest. What's this about?"

"First of all, I'd like to know where you were two nights ago."

His head tilted, he picked up a pen from the table and tapped it against his chin. "Ah, yes, I remember. I went for a drink. Is that against the law, Inspector?" His gleaming smile displayed perfectly white, even teeth.

"Not at all. Can you tell us where?"

"The Red Lion. Why?"

"Did you speak to anyone that night?"

He tutted and inhaled a large breath. "I speak to people all the time. I don't understand what the problem is."

"Can you remember talking to any *female* friends that night?"

"No."

"Really? We have CCTV footage which disputes that. Would you like to take a moment to rethink your answer, Mr. Hew?"

His mouth turned down at the sides. "No. Your question was: did I talk to any of my female friends that night. My answer remains the same. That's a negative, Inspector."

Sally's eyes narrowed at his smart reply. *I've got my work cut out with this one.* "Okay, let me rephrase my question then. Do you recall speaking to a female two nights ago?"

"Why, yes. I certainly do recall that pleasant event."

"Did you catch the lady's name you were having a conversation with?"

"Let me think." He clicked his fingers after a few moments' pause. "Gemma. I'm pretty sure she said her name was Gemma."

"Thank you for admitting that. Can you tell us what the conversation entailed?" Sally asked, her heart pounding against her ribs. She locked gazes with him.

"Life."

"Is that it?"

"We chatted about life in general. Nothing major really. It was just to fill in the time. I was standing at the bar and watched her go outside. She was an intriguing character."

"So your intention was to *chat* her up?"

"Hardly. She was wearing a wedding ring, not that it seems to count for much these days. In fact, married women can be worse than single girls for leading men on, in my humble opinion."

"Thanks for that insight. So, you spoke about life. Can you give me some idea how the conversation went?"

"Well, when I followed her into the children's play area, she appeared to be staring off into space. I startled her when I spoke; I didn't mean to scare her. She seemed fine after the initial interruption. She told me that she'd recently lost a friend to breast cancer and was contemplating her life."

Sally turned to Stuart. "Get this down, constable." Her partner's cheeks flared up, and he rummaged in his jacket pocket for his notebook and began to take notes. "Go on. Did she speak about her marriage at all?"

"Not really. I asked her what kind of career she had, and she informed me she was between jobs at present. The thing that puzzled me was she didn't seem downbeat about that fact when she mentioned it. She said she used to be a PA to a local businessman before she had her daughter. Like I say, it was just an ordinary chat, and we went our separate ways soon after."

"Why didn't you proceed with chatting her up, if you already knew she was married? Was it because she told you she had a child?"

"No. There really was nothing in it, Inspector. She was a pretty lady. That's about as far as I was willing to go with her at the end of the day." He frowned, and his eyes widened. "Shit! Wait just a damn minute. Has she told you otherwise? Am I being accused of doing something perverse with this woman? Because I'm telling you now, I never laid a bloody finger on her. Jesus, what is it with these women? The second a man shows interest in them, they're willing to scream 'rape.'"

Sally shook her head. "Now you're putting words into my mouth. This is a general enquiry as to what occurred the night before last when you spoke to Gemma Whiting. If your guilty conscience is pricking you, then that's your problem, not mine, Mr. Hew."

"It's not. I'm sorry for overreacting. It's just you hear so many of these cases getting to court, only to be dismissed by the judge as being lies told by the women. So where is all this leading to then, Inspector?"

"One last line of questioning before I reveal that, if you don't mind?"

He threw the pen down. It hit his coffee cup and bounced onto the floor. Ignoring it, he folded his arms. "Go on, let's get this over with."

"Okay, we've established where you were the night before last. Now I'd like you to tell me where you were last night. My constable was at your house first thing this morning, but received no reply. I'm assuming you stayed out all night. Is that correct?"

He unfolded his arms and applauded her. "Great deduction, Inspector. Don't tell me—it's an offence for a single man to stay out all night. Am I right?"

"I could do without the sarcasm, Mr. Hew. I'm investigating two very serious crimes, if you must know. Now, please just answer the question."

He flung his arms out to the side. "All right. I got lucky."

Sally's interest was piqued, and she raised an inquisitive eyebrow. "Care to fill me in on your conquest?"

"No. Not until you tell me what all this is about. I've been more than fair with you so far. It wouldn't hurt for you to let me know where this is leading, right?"

"*I* asked first. Just give me the name of the lady you spent the night with, and I'll walk away from here without asking further questions."

His eyes wandered the length of the busy road before he answered. He ran a hand under his collar and bit his lip nervously. "This is where it gets tricky."

"Oh? How so?" The way he was hesitating caused Sally great concern.

He fidgeted in his seat before finally admitting, "I was a naughty boy."

Sally sat upright. "Well, don't stop there, Mr. Hew. You've got my full attention."

He leaned forward. "It's hard for me to tell you this. Okay, I'm just going to let it out, but you have to promise me this won't go any further," he whispered.

"That's just it—I can promise no such thing without hearing the facts. You're going to have to trust me."

His eyes fluttered shut, and his jaw moved from side to side as he contemplated his dilemma. "I spent the night with a local dignitary's wife."

"Are you kidding me? Who? I need to corroborate your story with the lady herself before I let you off the hook. Name?"

"Jesus!" He scratched his head. "Clarissa Morgan."

Sally's eyebrows knitted together. "You mean, the local MP Patrick Morgan's wife?"

"Yes. Now can you understand my wanting—no, *needing*—to keep this quiet? He's out of town all week. She's going to bloody murder me if you wind up on her doorstep about this."

"We'll need to check your alibi all the same. I'm sorry if the shit is going to hit for you and Mrs. Morgan, but it's a necessity."

"Why? You have to tell me what this is all about, Inspector."

"For a start, a young lady is seriously ill in hospital after being attacked last night."

He gasped. "I would never harm a woman. What's that famous saying? Oh yes, 'I'm a lover, not a fighter'."

"And I have to tell you from the conversation we've had today, I'm inclined to believe you."

"Thank you. What about the other case? You mentioned there were two of them."

"Unfortunately, I have to inform you that the young lady you had a conversation with the night before last, was found murdered."

"What?" He sat forward in his chair, his eyes almost dropping onto the table in front of him. "My God. I don't believe it. How? Wait a minute, you suspected me of carrying out such a heinous crime?"

"At first, yes. However, now I'm willing to believe you had nothing to do with it. I'll need to verify your alibi with Mrs. Morgan, of course, but I can't see you divulging such a sensitive fact if you were guilty of these crimes. I will need to ask you to give me a DNA sample, if you don't mind? Just to omit you from our enquiries. Will you do that?"

"Of course. Holy crap. That poor woman, *women*. What a terrible situation. How could anyone take someone out like that?"

"Indeed, Mr. Hew. And you know what? Crimes like this are getting more and more prevalent by the day. Can you drop by the station later on today to give us that sample?"

"Around sixish. Will that do?"

"Perfect."

CHAPTER NINE

Sally watched the clock on the wall of the incident room tick its way around to four o'clock. At two minutes past four, she took the small file she had created on the suspect and walked down the stairs to the reception area. Peeping through the glass panel in the door, she saw Colin Whiting sitting nervously, awaiting her arrival. Her delay was intentional—she was eager to observe his reaction while he waited.

Sally entered the room and extended her hand for him to shake. He looked at it as though it were a cobra in disguise, ready to strike. "Mr. Whiting, sorry I'm late."

He stood up and shook her hand. "That's okay. Can we get this over with?"

"Of course." Sally turned to the desk sergeant and asked, "Got a spare constable who can sit in with us, Sergeant?"

"Will contact one now, ma'am."

"Send them through. We'll get settled." She led the way, and Whiting followed her up the hallway and into Interview Room One. "I'll be taping the conversation."

"Why? Am I under arrest?"

"No, it's a formality. I'll just set the machine up. Take a seat."

He pulled the chair out from the table and sat down heavily. He folded his arms and stared as she inserted the tape and waited for the PC to join them before she announced who was present in the room during the interview. "While we wait, I'd like to take a buccal swab for DNA purposes. Any objection?" Sally opened an envelope lying on the desk and removed a plastic tube.

Whiting fidgeted in his seat and glared at her. "Why do you need DNA?"

"It's normal. Nothing to be alarmed about. It's more for discounting someone from our enquiries. Is there a problem?"

His eyes latched on to hers, challenging her. "Nope, not at all."

As Sally inserted the large cotton bud into Whiting's mouth, the door opened, and a male PC walked into the room. Sally nodded and motioned for the constable to stand behind the suspect, against the wall of the ten-foot-square room. Then she concluded taking the sample and popped the evidence into the tube, sealed the envelope, and placed a sticker over the opening, on which she signed her name. "Thank you."

Sally said the obligatory words to begin the interview for the purpose of the tape and opened her file. "All right if I call you Colin?"

Whiting hitched up one of his shoulders. "Why not? It's my name."

"Good. Now, Colin, first of all, I'd like to take this opportunity to thank you for coming in this afternoon. I felt things were a little awkward when we spoke at your house yesterday. Can you explain why that was?"

"You'd just told me that my sister-in-law had died. How did you expect me to react, Inspector?"

"Fair point. So, can you tell me the reason you volunteered to come in today rather than discuss things in front of your wife?"

"Because I don't like talking about Gemma in front of Leona. They didn't really get on."

"That's strange. That isn't the impression I got from chatting to your wife. Care to tell me why they didn't get along?"

His eyes narrowed. Sally smiled, trying to fend off the glare coming at her in pulsating surges.

"You'll have to ask my wife that. Who knows what goes on in a woman's mind? I'm told it's a very complex muscle."

"I believe you're right about that, Colin. Okay, can you tell me what sort of relationship you had with Gemma?"

"Like any other brother and sister-in-law relationship, I suppose. There really wasn't anything special to it. I'll miss her; that's all I can tell you really. She was a superb mother to my niece, Samantha, and I'm sure my brother and his daughter will be lost without her."

"That's a great speech. You'll forgive me if I think you're just saying what you believe I want to hear, won't you?" Her smile never wavered.

"It happens to be the truth. I'm not sure I like your tone, Inspector. It's as if you're treating me as a suspect. May I remind you that I have come here today willingly?"

"Which I appreciate, Colin. The thing is, my team and I have been doing a little background check on all of the people concerned in this case, and something surprising turned up relating to an incident that occurred at a previous job you held."

"It was only a matter of time before that incident resurfaced and the finger started to get pointed in my direction. Maybe I should have been up-front from the word go about my conviction. It would have saved you a lot of time delving through my murky past, eh?"

"Maybe it would have made a difference. I've been told by a member of Gemma's family that they walked in on some kind of conflict going on between you and the deceased. Would you care to explain what that was about?" Sally intentionally used the word *deceased*, hoping to provoke further reaction from Whiting.

"And I can tell you exactly who placed those seeds of doubt in your head—Gemma's mum. Am I correct?"

"You might be. Care to enlighten me as to what the contretemps was about? Just so it's nice and clear in this complex mind of mine."

His gaze dropped to the table. His clutched his hands and began twisting as he contemplated what to say next. "Several things really."

"I'm listening," she prompted when he paused.

"Gemma and I used to be close, very close, in fact."

"As in you two had an affair?"

"Yes. But it didn't last."

"Why? What went wrong?" Sally asked, beginning to look at Colin in a different light. He seemed to be finally showing some true emotion about Gemma's death, as if it had just struck him. "Can I get you a glass of water?"

"No. I'm fine." He sniffed then let out a large sigh. "I loved her. But it wasn't reciprocated."

Whoa! Well, I hadn't expected that bolt of lightning. "Did anybody else know about your affair? Like her husband or your wife? Did either of them find out about it, Colin?"

"No. Gemma and I never told either of our spouses. It would have ripped the family apart."

"It's a pity you didn't think along those lines before you began the affair in the first place. Sorry, ignore me. Go on. Things must have been pretty strained between you in that case? Being in the same room as each other in front of the rest of the family, am I right?"

"Yes, but we coped. If you think I could kill Gemma, Inspector, you couldn't be further from the truth. I loved her, and I will continue to love her until I take my final breath in this world. She lit up a room when she entered it. There aren't many people in this life who that kind of statement can be attributed to, as I'm sure you'll agree."

"I agree. If that's the case, something has been puzzling me since our meeting at your house yesterday."

His gaze met hers again, and a furrowed brow signified his confusion. "What's that?"

"You never once asked how Gemma was killed. Why is that?"

He shook his head and expelled a huff. "I was devastated. Does the mind always function properly in such instances, Inspector? I'm sorry I didn't conform to how other family members took the news of Gemma's death. Like I say, I loved her."

"I can understand your feelings in that case. Can I ask who ended the affair?"

"She did."

"What were her reasons for that? Because she didn't love you in return?"

"Partially. She said that living with the guilt no longer sat well with her. I have to tell you that Mark and Gemma's marriage wasn't the rosiest around. Did you know that?"

"I'm getting the impression that there were problems within the marriage, yes. I have to tackle the case sensitively regarding Mark, as I'm sure you can appreciate. I will need to bring him in for questioning once things have settled down and he's had a chance to grieve the loss of his wife."

"I'm aware of that. I just wanted to be sure that you understood their marriage was rife with problems."

"Rife with problems? That bad? Or is that you having sour grapes?"

"Not at all. Mum has been intervening in their relationship for the last few months. She's threatened to bash their heads together on more than one occasion, at least once publicly, as far as I can remember."

"Then I better interview your mother to see if she can tell me what was at the root of their problems."

"You do that. Maybe that will finally get the heat off me. I swear, I had nothing to do with Gemma's death."

"Well, I'm sorry, but I had to bring you in for questioning. I hope you understand. To be fair, we're dealing with another similar incident in which the victim has survived."

"Really? Why didn't you tell me about this sooner? You've led me to believe that I'm your main suspect. All I'm guilty of is loving

Gemma. Did this victim give you any details about the person who attacked them?"

"No, not yet. She was badly hurt and is unconscious."

"But she's alive, unlike Gemma. Why hasn't there been some kind of warning issued about the attacks through the media? Surely it would be better to warn the women of Norfolk to be cautious."

"That's been taken care of this morning, Colin. There will be warnings going out over the next few days. It's another reason for me to take your DNA today so that you can be excluded from the second case."

"I understand. Do you need anything else from me?"

"Not at this time, Colin. All I ask is that you remain cooperative with us. It makes our life simpler if there is less testosterone flying around when we're investigating a case."

"Fair enough. Can I go now?"

Sally ended the interview and accompanied Colin back out into the car park. "My advice would be to lay low for a few days where your family is concerned. Mark will be hurting over the death of his wife, and if he hears any hint of what's gone on between you and Gemma, I dread to think how he'll react to the news."

"I'll keep my head down as advised. Any idea when Gemma's body will be released so that we can bury her?"

"I'll check that out for you over the next day or so. I need to drop your DNA off to the pathologist anyway. I might do that on my way home, actually. The last I heard, the funeral home had been in touch about collecting her body. I'll get back to you with a definitive answer tomorrow. How's that?"

"Thank you. I think the sooner we deal with Gemma's funeral, the better, for all our sakes."

He walked away, leaving Sally wondering what he'd meant by his last statement. Maybe she had been wrong to exclude him as a suspect so quickly after all. She nipped back to the interview room and picked up Colin's file and the DNA sample.

Sally intended to make two stops on her way home that evening: one to Clarissa Morgan's home and the other to the pathology department. After dispatching her team for the evening, she set off on her quest. As she approached her car, someone called out her name. She twisted to see who was addressing her.

"Ah, Mr. Hew. Right on time, I see."

"As requested, Inspector."

"Okay, I'll deal with your DNA sample before I head home for the evening." She walked back into the station alongside him and asked the desk sergeant for another DNA kit. He dipped under the counter and produced an envelope. "Can you ask another PC to join me in an interview room for five minutes, Sergeant?"

"I'll organise that immediately, ma'am."

"Walk this way, Mr. Hew."

Sally waited for the PC to join them then went through the same procedure she'd gone through with Colin Whiting to obtain the sample from Taylor Hew. After completing that undertaking, she left the building again and thanked Mr. Hew for turning up on time. Then she placed both DNA samples on her passenger seat and drove to the pathology department.

Simon was emerging from his theatre, still in his uniform, when she walked up the hallway towards his office.

"Just the man I want to see."

"Give me five minutes to get some decent clothes on first, Sally." She nodded.

"You can wait in my office, no problem."

Sally sighed heavily as she sat in the spare chair. It had been a long day already, and she still had another stop to make before going home. Withdrawing her mobile from her jacket pocket, she dialled her parents' home. "Hi, Mum. I should be home by about seven."

"Okay, dear. See you later."

Puzzled, Sally was still looking down at her phone when Simon walked into the office, dressed in civvies.

"What's wrong?"

"I haven't got a clue. Just rang Mum to let her know what time I'll be home this evening and received a response that I wasn't really expecting, as if she was distant about something. Oh, well, I'm sure I'll find out soon enough."

Simon sniggered. "Don't tell me you're still living at home?"

"Out of necessity—both my parents' and my own. Don't ask. It suits all concerned." Sally nodded at the two sample envelopes she'd placed on his desk. "I've got two samples for you. One is from Colin Whiting. I've just pulled him in for questioning and discovered that he had an affair with Gemma behind his brother's back."

"Nice family. Could he be the father of her child? Is that what you're thinking?"

Sally chewed her lip. "I hope not, for all their sakes. I don't think they're the most loving of families. That sort of news could do irreparable damage, even if the mother and child are no longer with us."

"And who does the other sample belong to?"

"The man, a stranger, who spoke to Gemma. He's one of the last people to see her alive on the evening of her death."

"I see. So you're looking at trying to match his DNA to anything found at the murder scene in that case, as opposed to the child's DNA?"

"That's right. I think he's innocent, but you know as well as I do, there's just no telling today. Criminals are getting craftier by the day. I'm going to shoot off now. Can I have the DNA match to the baby's ASAP?"

"I'll order the lab to treat it as a priority. I'll try and get an answer for you in the next twenty-four to forty-eight hours. How's that?"

"You're a star. Thanks, Simon." Sally stood and walked towards the door. "Have a good evening."

"You, too. I hope all is well when you get home with your mother."

"Me, too."

Sally left the pathology department and drove to Clarissa Morgan's address. At first, the woman objected profusely to Sally showing up at her home, but with her husband's arrival imminent, she told Sally what she wanted to know about the illicit night she'd spent with Taylor Hew. The meeting took all of ten minutes once the woman succumbed and revealed the truth.

When Sally arrived at her parents' home, Dex greeted her in his usual enthusiastic way of going around and around in circles, before finally collapsing on the floor for a tummy rub. "Hello, treasure. I'm glad to see you, too." She kissed the top of his head, and he let out a groan of pleasure. "Maybe we'll have time to squeeze in a run down by the river later, eh?"

"That'll be nice, love. Hard day, I take it?" Her father's voice startled her.

Sally patted Dex's tummy then kissed her father on the cheek and gave him a weary smile. "You could say that, Dad. I've been racing the length and breadth of the county today. What about you? Any news on that contract you quoted on?"

"Not yet, love. I'm sure I'll hear by the end of the week."

Sally linked arms and ventured into her mother's sacred domain the kitchen. "Can I help with anything, Mum?"

"Hello, dear. I'm fine. Your father has already laid the table." Her mother wiped a hand across her eyes.

Sally winked at her father and motioned for him to leave them alone. He nodded and called Dex into the back garden.

Sally's mother glanced her way. Seeing the redness around her mother's eyes upset Sally. "Mum, what's wrong?"

"I don't know, love. I keep bursting into tears when I least expect it."

Sally took the wooden spoon from her mother's hand and directed her over to the kitchen table. "Mum, sit there. I'll finish the dinner."

"No, that's not fair. You've been out at work all day. I'll be fine, love."

"Come on. What's really going on, Mum? You can confide in me. Are you and Dad having marital problems?" She stirred the gravy as it came to a boil. Her mother's silence made her turn her head sharply. "Mum?"

Her mother had pulled a tissue from the nearby box and was wiping fresh tears from her eyes. "It's really nothing to worry about. We're fine, in our own way."

Sally switched off the gas beneath the vegetables and marched across the room. She sat next to her mother and clasped her hands between her own. "You can't say that and expect me not to ask what you mean, Mum. Are you having marriage problems? Is it the debt situation?"

"No, that's sorted now, thanks to your generous gesture." Her mother waved a hand in front of her. "Just ignore me. I'm feeling emotional, and I have no idea why."

"Is it the menopause? Maybe your body has got used to the tablets you're on. Perhaps you need to visit the doc's to get a check-up. Do you want me to come with you?"

"Men have no idea what we bloody have to contend with, do they? I get a sudden whoosh go right through me, as if a cauldron has been set alight in my stomach, and it erupts throughout my body. I can't describe the feeling any better than that. I hope you never have to go through it, darling."

"That's terrible, Mum. Maybe you should try and pinpoint when these sudden rushes come on. I read an article the other month about some studies scientists have conducted recently about the effects of caffeine on a menopausal woman. I'll see if I can find it for you to read. Take it to the doc's with you and get his opinion on the report."

"Perhaps I'll limit my intake for a week or so, just to see if there's any truth in it. All I can say is that when these surges strike, God help you and your father if you're within reach. I'm warning you now—I'm not totally in control of my faculties when they occur. Take cover. Maybe you both should consider wearing tin hats for your own protection."

Sally leaned over and kissed her mother's cheek, noticing the heat beneath her lips when she brushed her mother's skin. "You're burning up, Mum. I'm going to call the doc's first thing, get you an appointment. It'll probably be a couple of weeks before he can fit you in anyway."

"I'll make the call; I promise. You have enough on your plate as it is, love. How's the case going?"

"Cases! They're going. I found out today that the first victim who died was pregnant."

Her mother gasped and covered her mouth. Clasping her hands together on the table once more, she said, "Just goes to show that there's always someone worse off than yourself, doesn't it? I must stop wallowing in self-pity. I have a loving husband and a beautiful, talented daughter. What more could a person want in life?"

"I thought the same thing, Mum. Apparently, this young lady had everything to live for. Now she's going to be six feet under in a matter of days. Life's so unfair. It should be a lesson to us all to live life to the full and to always be grateful for the hand we've been dealt. I know that I've changed my perception on life since dumping Darryl, and I have to say, I feel a whole lot better for doing that, too."

"You're remarkable. I'm in awe of the way you handled that situation. I'm not sure how I would have coped if I were confronted with the same horrendous ordeal you had to go through. Let's hope the judge is female and comes down on your side in the trial, love."

"I really don't want to think about that now. We'll find out soon enough. Hey, I'm starving. Is that dinner ready yet?" Sally smiled and placed a hand on her mother's cheek. "I love you, Mum. Don't ever change. So what if the menopause makes you fly off the handle now and again? It won't make Dad or me feel any differently towards you. Just give us fair warning, and we'll all survive to live another day."

"I love you, too, sweetheart. I couldn't wish for a lovelier daughter. And yes, dinner is ready to be served up now. Do you want to help?"

They left the table, their arms wrapped around each other's waist, as the back door opened. Her father was waving a white hanky tied to a garden cane. "Is it safe for us men to come in now?" he asked, referring to himself and Dex.

Sally and her mother burst into laughter. "I think that's acceptable. Don't you, Mum?"

"For now. Make the most of it. Not sure when Vesuvius will erupt again. I'm sorry for having a go at you, Christopher."

Her father joined them and placed his arms around them both. "Group hug. No need to apologise, Janine. I love you all the same."

Sally smiled lovingly at her parents, and a pang of envy tugged at her heart when she realised she would never experience the true companionship her parents shared because of the scars one man had left on her life. *Damn you, Darryl Parker. I hope the judge locks you up for years for the heartache you've triggered within me. Shame on you and all the other men in this world who refuse to treat women as their equals.*

After dinner and all the clearing up was completed, Sally made good on her promise to take Dex for a walk down by the river, before it grew dark. She watched the golden-haired lab bounding through the long grass, stalking the birds, and barking at them as they took flight. Life was good when she was out with her treasured friend. Her mobile rang. She took the phone out of her pocket and groaned. "Hi, Jack. You beat me to it; I was about to ring you. How's Teresa doing?"

"Hi, Sally. Well, she's delivered the baby—it's a girl, by the way—but there are complications with the little one."

"Oh, sweetie, I'm so sorry to hear that. Is it because of the baby's size?"

"Partially, plus they think she has a heart defect. They're going to carry out further tests in the next few days. After all the turmoil we've been through over the last few months, it looks like it will all be in vain if the little mite doesn't pull through."

She could hear the tremor in her partner's voice. "Hey, Bullet, don't you dare give up on that girl. Think positive. They're stronger than people give them credit for at times—even I know that. Hang in there. Promise me?"

"I will. But the doc has told us not to raise our hopes. If I think positive, it's only going to make it a darn sight worse when the day comes to say goodbye to the little one, won't it?"

"Bloody hell! I'm sorry, Jack. Hey, the doc might be wrong. Don't write her off just yet. How's Teresa feeling?"

"Sore. She won't stop crying, which is understandable. Her mother's reacting very much the same way. I feel a right shit not joining them."

"Don't be daft. I can hear how upset you are. They'll realise how inadequate you feel, I'm sure. They probably appreciate your strength not to break down right now. Don't be too despondent, matey."

"Thanks, boss. You've hit the nail on the head, it's the feeling of inadequacy that's hard to handle. Needless to say, I'd like to take the day off tomorrow, if that's okay?"

"Of course. Take all the time you need. I'll drop by the chief's office tomorrow to let him know. Give my love to the girls. Ring me with any developments, you hear me? Take care."

"Will do. Thanks, Sally."

She hung up and called Dex. Dropping to her knees, she cuddled and kissed the dog on the head. "I'm so glad I have you, boy. Come on, let's go home before it gets dark." She placed the slip leash over his head, and they walked back to the house just as nightfall descended.

CHAPTER TEN

Sally smiled when she heard her mother singing as she prepared breakfast for them all the following morning. "You sound much happier, Mum. You're challenging the birds with that beautiful dawn chorus." She kissed her mother on the cheek and let Dex out the back door.

"Maybe there's some truth in that old adage about a problem shared, after all, darling. I can't thank you enough for the support you've shown me over my menopause. Not everyone would be as understanding as you and your father. I'm blessed to have you both in my life."

Sally sniggered and poured them all a cup of tea. "Just remember *that* the next time the urge to attack us with a frying pan takes your fancy, okay?"

"I'll do that, dear. The menopause is loathsome! If I could suck all my productive bits out, I would!"

"Mum! You are funny."

Her mother studied her with a perturbed expression. "Are you mocking me, child?"

"Don't be silly. I bet thousands of women in your situation feel the same."

Her mother smiled and touched Sally's face gently. "You're one in a million, daughter of mine... one in a million. Do you have time for scrambled eggs on toast?"

"Try and stop me, as long as I can have it with lashings of ketchup. I can't eat eggs without disguising them. You know that."

"That peculiarity of yours has never wavered over the years."

Her father entered the kitchen and pecked them both on the cheek. "How are my two favourite girls this morning?"

"Full of the joys of spring, except it's the middle of September. Work that one out, Dad." Sally chortled.

"That's good to hear. I could eat two horses this morning, Janine. What's on the menu, love?"

Her mother chuckled. "The things that come out of a chicken's bum. Will that do you?"

Sally laughed at her father's shocked expression and sought out the cutlery to lay the breakfast table.

Her father let out a huff. "I'm beginning to regret asking. Yuck! What a bloody image that just conjured up."

It was wonderful to share a pleasant, angst-free breakfast with her parents before she said farewell to them and set off for the station.

When she pushed open the doors to the incident room, Sally found the rest of the team already busy at their desks. She glanced up at the clock on the wall to see it was only five minutes to eight. Her chest puffed out with pride for her team's willingness to attack their day before their shift began. "You guys rock… just saying."

"You set a good example… just saying." Joanna smiled. She looked up from her computer, and her face turned serious. "Any news on Jack's daughter, boss?"

"I'm sure he won't mind you guys knowing. The news isn't good, I'm afraid. The little mite has a desperate fight ahead of her. She was born with a heart defect. Needless to say, Jack will be absent for a few days. That reminds me—I need to make the chief aware of the situation first thing. Anything useful turn up from the TV appeal aired last night?"

"A few things. Mainly to do with the second attack. I'll make some notes and let you have them in a couple of minutes, boss," Joanna said.

"Sounds positive. Okay, I'll be right back." Sally inhaled a few calming breaths as she walked along the corridor to the chief's office. DCI Green's secretary was busy putting filter paper in the coffee machine when she walked in the office. "Fresh coffee—you can't beat it, Lyn, can you? Is he in?"

"He is, and no, you can't beat fresh coffee. The smell perks me up instantly when the machine starts churning early in the morning. Have you seen Joan recently?"

Sally smiled as her previous chief's warm features filled her mind. Joan Cradley had retired from the force almost two years before, and DCI Mick Green had filled her shoes less than adequately in Sally's mind. But then, to be fair, Sally could have been biased, as she and Joan had become firm friends over the years. Being a high-ranking female copper in a man's world always took its toll, though. In the end, the stress of the job had culminated in Joan bowing out and taking retirement in her early fifties. Since then, Sally had remained in contact with Joan and had visited her on a few occasions in her new home out in the sticks, tucked away from all civilian life. One of Sally's other female copper friends, Lorne Warner, had gone down the same route at an early age. Although, in

Lorne's case, her calling to be a copper had drawn her back into the Met soon after she'd opted to take early retirement. The force was in her blood, and Sally totally comprehended that sentiment. She had no idea what she would do if ever she were forced to leave her beloved Norfolk Constabulary. Sally shook the thought from her head and replied, "Sorry. Drifted off then for a second, envious of Joan's life in her tranquil setting. I haven't spoken to her for about a month. You?"

"I rang her at the weekend. She's deliriously happy about having yet another granddaughter to coo over."

"How wonderful. Is it really nine months since she told us about that? I hate the way time is passing us by so quickly."

"I was amazed by the announcement, too. She asked after you, specifically about the court case. That's coming up soon, isn't it?"

Sally's mouth twisted. "Did you have to remind me? Two weeks, to be honest. The nerves are beginning to jangle a little. It's one thing bringing the bastard to court; it's another thing having to face him in the dock, his eyes eating into your flesh. Oops, that's a tad melodramatic."

"Will you take someone with you on the day for moral support? I'll volunteer if you need someone to hold your hand, Sally."

"That's kind of you, Lyn. I think—I hope—Mum and Dad will be there with me."

The chief's office door opened, and he looked daggers at both of them. "Could we possibly leave the gossiping until lunchtime, ladies? I have a huge pile of correspondences I need to get my head around first thing. That's a little difficult with you nattering away out here."

Sally winked at Lyn, whose cheeks had flared up. "My fault, sir. Do you have five minutes?"

He pushed open the door and stepped back for Sally to join him. He closed the door behind them, marched past her, and reclaimed his seat behind his large mahogany desk. "What's this in connection with, Inspector?"

"I wanted to let you know that I've given my partner permission to take a few days off, sir."

His brow wrinkled heavily. "In the middle of a big case? Is that wise?"

"No, but a necessity all the same, sir. His daughter has just given birth to his first grandchild, and it's touch and go whether the baby makes it." His brow relaxed, and he reclined in his chair, linking his hands together on the desk. "Compassion won through in the end, sir."

"I understand. Well, I hope the baby survives. That must be a horrendous situation to contend with. How is the case proceeding?"

Sally was tempted to shake her head in disgust at the way the chief appeared to change the subject so quickly. Instead, she relented and sighed heavily. "Well, I'm just about to go through the calls we've received from the appeal that went out last night. I've interviewed a few people concerning the first crime, the murder, and I have to say, although I have one or two suspects in mind, we have no evidence as such to fling at the suspects as yet. However, the pathologist rang me yesterday to say the victim was four weeks pregnant, and I also learned that she had an affair with her brother-in-law."

"I see. So, that's clearly the motive."

"I'd rather get the DNA evidence to back up any accusations, sir. I should have that on my desk either today or tomorrow. It's certainly a step forward in the investigation and one that could possibly lead in either of two directions."

"How so?"

"Either the husband or his brother could be the murderer. At least, that's my line of thinking after contemplating the case throughout the night."

"You make a valid point, Inspector. So if the DNA evidence regarding the foetus comes back as unexpected, I take it you'll be arresting the brother-in-law."

"I'll certainly be instructing him to come in for further questioning. Not sure I'm ready to go out on a limb and arrest him for simply fathering an unborn child, sir."

"Nonsense, Inspector. That's a motive right there—he's killed her in order to prevent her from telling everyone about their affair."

"I understand where you're coming from, sir, but the husband might have found out she was playing away from home. If so, there's every possibility that he killed his wife in a violent rage. By what I can gather, the marriage was in jeopardy."

"Ah, well, that certainly throws a different light on things. I totally understand your dilemma. Let's hope the DNA helps to make things a lot clearer for you. What if the DNA belongs to neither of these men?"

Sally's eyes widened. "Crap, I never really thought about that, sir. That would make the investigation spin out of control, upside down, and on its head. I'd rather not think about that now. I better get on with the investigation, sir. I just dropped by to inform you of Jack's predicament."

"Very well. Do you have a suitable replacement for him within your team?"

"Oh yes, sir, any member of my team is capable of stepping up to the plate. They wouldn't totally fill the void, but I reckon eighty percent would be covered."

"Glad to hear it, that's as it should be. Keep me informed of your progress as usual, Inspector."

"I will, sir."

Sally walked out of the office and rested against the closed door. She exhaled a large breath as her heart rate recovered to near normal. Leaning forward, she whispered, "Why do I always feel as if I've been placed on the naughty step every time I enter this room?"

Lyn chortled. "I totally understand that. He's a pussycat really, once you get to know him."

Sally snorted and walked towards the outer door of the office. "I'll have to take your word on that, Lyn. He has a tendency to bite my hand off every time I go to stroke him, metaphorically speaking of course."

Lyn laughed, and Sally shook her head. "Christ, did I really say that out loud? I'm more stressed out than I thought. Have a good day."

"You, too."

Sally marched back to the incident room and headed in Joanna's direction. "I know it's only been a few minutes, but have you got anything useful for me?"

"A few things, boss. I've put them in order of priority." Joanna handed Sally a sheet of paper just as her phone rang. "Hello, DC Tryst. How can I help?"

Sally scanned the sheet, admiring the way Joanna had prioritised the list, just as Sally would have herself. That task alone boded well for the constable's future on the team, not that Sally had ever doubted the young woman's capabilities in the first place. She looked up to see Joanna beaming.

"Thanks for letting me know. We'll send a team out there immediately. Goodbye."

"What was that?" Sally asked, cocking her head.

"Julie Smith has regained consciousness and is sitting up in bed."

Sally dropped the list on the desk and pointed at Joanna. "Great news. You're coming with me to the hospital."

"Really? How fabulous. Thanks, boss."

CHAPTER ELEVEN

Numerous times during the drive, Sally found herself wondering if she'd been right to invite the young detective constable to be her partner for the morning. If there had been a gold medal in the art of chatting enthusiastically about every conceivable topic under the sun, Joanna would have won it hands down. Sally nodded and voiced lots of yeses at the appropriate times, not wishing to dampen Joanna's passion by chastising her. However, when Sally parked the car in the hospital car park, she felt obliged to guide the constable's train of thought back to the task in hand.

"So, here's the plan. We take things nice and slowly, okay?"

"Yes, boss. Do you want me to take notes?"

"That's a definite requirement when you're out in the field with me, Joanna. Leave the questions to me, too, all right?"

"Of course." Joanna beamed at her.

"Let's go then." Sally led the way to the ICU and produced her warrant card for the nurse sitting at the reception desk. "The station received a call saying that Julie Smith had regained consciousness. Is she up to answering a few questions?"

The petite redhead smiled and motioned for them to take a seat, which Sally declined. "I'll certainly ask the question for you. The doctor is examining her now." The nurse left the desk and slipped into the room. A few minutes later, she returned with the doctor.

"My patient is still feeling very fragile, Inspector, but when I asked her if she felt up to seeing you, she swiftly agreed."

"That's wonderful news. How is Julie's health, Doctor?"

"Her injuries appear to be healing rapidly. Some patients have the ability to do that. Go easy on her, all the same. Although we've carried out a few basic tests, we're unsure what limits there are with her memory as yet."

"You have my word on that, Doc."

The doctor returned to the unit and held open the door for Sally and Joanna to join him. Julie Smith immediately looked their way. Her head was still wrapped in bandages, and the bruising on her face was even more evident than it had been the first time Sally had visited her.

Sally smiled and introduced herself and Joanna. "Hello, Julie. Daft question in the circumstances, but how are you feeling?"

Julie's eyes fluttered shut then reopened again as she sucked in a large breath. "Glad to still be alive, I suppose."

"That's the ticket. Are you up to telling us what happened?"

"I can try. Not sure I'll be much help, really. The attacker struck out at me before I realised what had gone on."

"I understand. Did you get a good look at him? Are there any details you can give us?"

"My memory appears to be reluctant to revisit the actual attack at the moment, Inspector."

Sally raised her hand. "There's no rush. Take your time. Can you close your eyes for me? I'll try and walk through the scene with you. Remember, I'm only a few steps away."

Again, Julie inhaled a large breath and allowed her eyes to close slowly. Sally watched as a pained expression contorted the woman's young features during the process.

"Where are you, Julie?"

"I'm walking down Chester Road. I've just left my friends at the pub, and no, I'm not drunk." The briefest of smiles tugged at her lips but vanished when she took up her story once again. "He walked towards me. It was dark. I was looking down at the ground, avoiding eye contact. I shuddered. I thought it was because of the evening chill, but I think I sensed some form of danger." Her eyes flew open.

Sally reached over and patted the back of her hand. "Take your time. There's really no need to rush, Julie. Can I get you a glass of water?"

"Yes, thank you."

Sally moved round the bed to the water jug and glass. She handed the young woman a half-filled glass, and Julie accepted it with a shaking hand. "Relax. The last thing I want to do is hamper your recovery. If you don't feel able to continue today, that's fine by me."

"No. I want to do it—if you're prepared to be patient with me. You need to catch this man before he hurts someone else."

"Exactly. In your own time. So you were walking, not driving?"

Julie clung to the glass with both hands and closed her eyes once more. "That's right. He's much taller than me. I'm five-foot-three. He looked about six feet tall." She sipped the water again and swallowed noisily.

"What's he wearing?"

"Black jeans, I think. It's hard to tell because of the dark. Yes, I think they're black. He's also wearing a grey hoodie."

"Can you make out his physique? Is he slim, or is he carrying a little excess weight?"

"He's very thin. If it was a girl, I'd put her at borderline anorexic." Julie opened her eyes and looked uncertainly at Sally as if needing reassurance.

"You're doing really well. You've given us a lot of information already," Sally said, unsure whether she would be able to give the same level of detail if she'd been in the victim's shoes.

Julie closed her eyes again and squeezed them tightly. Her grip tightened around the glass of water at the same time. "I think he growled at me. I kept my head down, didn't want to alienate him at all. There was no one else around. No one would hear me if I cried out for help..."

"Take a breather. Don't get stressed out, Julie."

But Julie refused to stop. Her breath came out in short sharp bursts.

Sally glanced at the doctor, who was watching Julie's vital signs rise on the monitor, but he seemed reluctant to intervene. Sally took that to mean he didn't feel the patient was in any immediate danger. However, she decided to continue cautiously. "As soon as he passed, I felt his arms grip me, constricting my movements. There was an alley close by..."

"Did he take you to the alley?"

"I was in shock. Frozen in fear. My throat seized up. By then, I couldn't cry out, then his hand covered my mouth to prevent me. He was strong, very strong. It confused me because he didn't look as though he'd have the strength to drag me, but he did. It seemed a lifetime swept by before I could react. I kicked out, tried to trip him up. I used to be enrolled in a judo class when I was in my teens. Everything I learned in these lessons escaped me momentarily. Slowly, the moves came flooding back. I thrashed out, tried to throw him off me. I must have pissed him off, because he hurled me to the ground."

"Is that how your head got injured, Julie?"

"I think so. Wait..." She squeezed her eyes together, tighter than before.

"What is it? What do you see?"

"He beat me. Kept thumping me in the face. His hood tipped back. I can clearly see the whites of his eyes now." She shuddered, and teardrops seeped onto her cheek.

"Can you see the colour of his hair, Julie?"

"It's black. Tightly knitted. Oh my God, he's black! Yes, I can see him clearly now."

The words hit Sally as if a boxer had struck a knockout blow. It was crystal clear in that instant that Julie's and Gemma's attackers might not have been the same person. Gemma's family members were at the top of their suspect list—and none of them were black. "Are you one hundred percent certain, Julie?"

"As sure as I'm going to get, Inspector. He was definitely black and painfully thin for a man, with the strength of a raging bull."

"That really helps us a lot. What about if I sent a police artist in to see you? Do you think you'd be able to go into further detail?"

"Things are becoming clearer all the time. If you leave it until tomorrow, maybe I'll be able to give you even more details. I can't promise anything, though."

Sally looked in the doctor's direction for authorisation. He nodded his acceptance. She patted Julie's hand again. "That's wonderful news. Try and get some rest now. Thank you for pushing yourself to the limit in order to give us vital information. I'll send an artist in tomorrow afternoon. How's that?"

"Okay, hopefully, providing I don't have a relapse in the meantime, I should be okay to give the artist a detailed description. I'll try and jot things down if anything else comes to mind during the day. I want you to catch this man quickly. He's a danger to other women out there, Inspector."

"I'm sure we will arrest him soon, with your help. I hope your recuperation goes well. Thank you for your assistance. I'll be in touch shortly."

"I'm glad I could be helpful. Sorry I couldn't provide you with more detail."

"You've given us a great start, Julie."

The doctor escorted Sally and Joanna off the ward. "Thank you, Doctor. I know you had your reservations back there, yet you allowed the interview to continue. I appreciate that."

"I was keeping a watchful eye on her vitals. I'm glad she's supplied you with enough details to arrest the attacker. Let the nurse know when the artist will be coming in, okay?"

"I will. Thank you."

Sally and Joanna began the twisting journey through the hospital corridors back to the car. "Interesting morning's work, eh, Joanna? Especially as I was originally told the incident took place on a country lane."

"So it would appear, boss. You're thinking that we're looking for two different assailants. Am I right?"

"Spot on. There's nothing similar in the cases at all. However, we still need to be vigilant and not become complacent. I need to make a call to the pathology department before we do anything else."

Once settled in the car, Sally rang the lab. "Simon, it's Sally Parker. I know it's a bit early, but do you have any news for me?"

"Actually, I saw something on my desk with reference to your case when I came in. I've been in a PM for the past hour. Now where did I put it? Ah… here it is…"

Sally heard the sound of papers being shuffled, and the pathologist tutted and cursed under his breath before he came back on the line. "I hope you're sitting down for this, Inspector."

"I am. I'm in the car outside the hospital, which I'll tell you about later. Hit me with it."

"It would appear that the child Gemma was carrying belonged to Colin Whiting."

"I had my suspicions. There's no possibility of mistaking his DNA with his brother's?"

"You know better than to ask that."

"Yeah, I'm just covering all the angles, Simon."

"May I ask why you're at the hospital? Is it to do with the case?"

"The new case, yes. Julie Smith has regained consciousness and given us a brief description of the man who attacked her."

"Interesting. And? Don't leave me dangling."

"Well, she seemed to think the man who attacked her was black, which leads me to believe that the two cases aren't connected."

"None of the suspects in the Whiting case are black?"

"That's right. I don't suppose you've managed to find any DNA connecting the crime scenes yet?"

"No, nothing. But then we wouldn't if your assumption proves to be correct. Well, I must crack on. I'll e-mail this report over to you so you have a copy on file."

Sally hung up and placed her hands on the steering wheel. "You were expecting that result, boss. Weren't you?"

She turned to face Joanna. "I was. Nonetheless, it's still come as a bit of a shock. The question is, what do I do about it?"

Joanna frowned. "Arrest Colin Whiting?"

"On what charge? Getting his brother's wife up the duff? While it's immoral, it's not actually an arrestable offence. Although we could bring him in for further questioning in relation to the evidence, it could be deemed as a possible motive. Sticky ground, though, considering we have no evidence placing him, or anyone else for that matter, at the scene."

"I understand. Maybe it would have been better not finding out that snippet of information."

"It is certainly going to hamper my line of thinking. The clue is too substantial to ignore or to confront head on." She slapped the steering wheel with the palm of her hand. "What are we missing? Maybe I should question some of her friends again. I know they've already been seen, but not by me. Perhaps they can tell us how the affair started, if they were aware of it at all. Either way, I don't want to reveal the truth to the family yet while they're grieving." She tutted. "There again, I do think Gemma's mother has the right to know. Bugger, I'm damned if I do and damned if I don't."

"Eek... I don't envy you, boss. Why don't we leave it for now and see what other information comes in during the course of the day from the TV appeal?"

Sally nodded and smiled at the constable. "That makes a lot of sense, Joanna."

The first task Sally adopted when she got back to the station was to arrange for the police artist to visit Julie Smith that afternoon. Being armed with some form of positive description of the assailant meant they could check the national computer for a match. Sally decided to appoint Jordan as the lead on Julie's case.

By lunchtime, Sally was feeling frustrated by the lack of calls they'd received after the TV appeal. She sent Joanna out to buy sandwiches for the team, and together they spent the next few hours tracking down and talking to Gemma's friends who were with her the night of her death. Sally looked out the window of her office. Her stomach churned when she looked over the results. Not one of Gemma's friends could shed any light about an affair between

Gemma and Colin. *Isn't that the sort of thing one confides to a best friend? Why didn't Gemma? What does this mean?*

If Gemma's friends weren't aware, then maybe her mother was. Sally rang Heather Lord and arranged to visit her at three o'clock that afternoon. Again, Sally took Joanna along. "Be prepared for her mother breaking down. Take notes when necessary."

"Yes, boss."

Heather was waiting for them on the doorstep of her home. The poor woman looked a mess. Her hair was uncombed, and the dark circles around her bloodshot eyes told Sally that the woman's mourning had taken a toll on her ability to sleep.

Smiling weakly, Heather welcomed them into her home. "I was a little surprised to hear from you so soon, Inspector. Hopefully, you're bringing me some good news."

Sally sighed heavily and bit her lip. "Maybe we should take a seat first, Heather."

"Can I get you a drink?"

Sally and Joanna declined the offer. "I do have some news for you. I wanted to tell you the news in person rather than over the phone. I imagine that it's going to be somewhat difficult for you to hear."

Heather gulped noisily. "Whatever is the matter? Do you know who robbed me of my beautiful daughter?"

"Not yet."

"Then I don't understand what you're getting at, Inspector. You're worrying me. Please, just tell me what you've discovered?"

"First of all, I need to ask you about your daughter's relationship with her husband."

"As I've told you already, they had their ups and downs. Is Mark the main suspect? Is that what you're here to tell me?"

"No. I just wanted to get further insight into their marriage."

"All I can tell you is that things have been strained in that household for a few months now—why? I have no idea. My daughter refused to tell me."

"Why? Weren't you close?"

"Yes, very close. Maybe she thought I'd go round there and interfere. I've been known to let rip on occasion."

"And would you have?" Sally asked, tilting her head.

Heather shrugged. "A mother should always do what she can to protect her child. I'm no different in that respect."

"I've asked Gemma's friends if they knew about your daughter's marriage difficulties, and I have to say that the news came as a shock to most of them, which strikes me as a little odd."

"Do *you* tell your friends every detail of your life, Inspector? Maybe Gemma confided in Melinda more than her other friends."

Sally winced when she thought about the huge secret she'd kept from her own good friends regarding Darryl's abusive tendencies. Everyone had disbelieved her at first when she'd told them she'd been forced to arrest her own husband. "Maybe. I don't think we've contacted Melinda. Was she out with the group the other night?"

Heather shook her head. "No. Sadly, she lost her battle against breast cancer a few months ago. She was Gemma's best friend. I pray to God that she was waiting for Gemma to complete her journey to the other side."

"I'm sorry to hear that. I hope she was there, too," Sally replied, not really one for believing in that kind of mumbo jumbo.

"You mentioned some news you have for me."

Sally looked the woman in the eye and nodded. "The post-mortem results are back, and they have thrown up a surprising outcome."

"What's that?" Heather asked, sitting forward in her chair.

"Were you aware that Gemma was pregnant?"

Heather's shoulders slumped, and her mouth dropped open. "How far gone?"

"About four weeks. You had no idea, I take it?"

"No." Tears poured from her eyes; she wiped them away on the back of her hand, but a steady stream of fresh tears replaced them. She started rocking back and forth on the edge of her seat and stared at a swirl of pattern in the carpet. "I never knew. I doubt she knew, either. She wouldn't have kept that kind of news a secret from me."

"Do you know if Gemma and Mark were trying for another baby?"

"I don't think so. She would have told me. I think Samantha was more than either of them were able to cope with."

Sally chewed on the inside of her mouth for a second or two before she delivered the news she anticipated would rock the woman's world off its axis. "I actually found out about the pregnancy yesterday, but the investigation has been full-on for the last twenty-four hours, as you can imagine. Anyway, after questioning a few suspects, I acquired DNA samples from the men in question. I asked the pathologist to match the DNA to the sample of the foetus as a long shot."

"And? Who were the suspects?" Heather sniffled.

"I can't really tell you that. I just want you to be aware that we do have someone on our radar."

"But that's not fair. Surely as Gemma's mother, I have a right to know who you think the suspect is." She gasped. "It *is* a member of that family, isn't it? If not Mark, then…"

"I can't tell you, I'm sorry. All will be revealed soon enough. I just wanted you to be aware of Gemma's pregnancy more than anything."

Heather's face drained of all colour. She couldn't have looked more stunned if Sally had thrown a bucket of cold water over her head. "That's like only telling me half the story, Inspector."

"I know. Again, I apologise. Over the next few days, maybe we'll gain enough information to address that situation. Until then, I have to keep the suspect's name under wraps. Please understand that, Heather."

"I can't believe this. Will you tell Mark, or have you told him already?"

"No. To be honest, I would rather keep the details hush-hush for now."

"Why?"

"He's just lost his wife, which is a devastating experience in itself. If I went over there and told him that Gemma was carrying a baby when she died, how do you think he's going to react to that? He needs time to grieve for his wife. The only reason I have decided to tell you is because I promised you that I would keep you informed on how the case progressed. I'm relying on you to keep this information between us for now, Heather."

"I really don't understand that, Inspector." She gasped.

"What is it?" Sally asked.

"I know you haven't named the father, but if it's Colin, do you think this is what the contretemps between Gemma and Colin was about?"

"Again, I can't speculate on that at present. When did the contretemps take place? In August? Can you remember the date exactly?"

"Not without looking at the calendar." She crossed the room to the calendar standing upright on the cabinet and picked it up.

Pointing, she counted back the weeks. "I think it was around the sixteenth of August."

"Well, it's September seventeenth today, which just tallies at a stretch with what the pathologist told us. He thought Gemma was only four weeks pregnant."

"It has to be him, Inspector. He must be the one who killed my daughter. Perhaps he had an inkling that she was pregnant. Maybe they were using contraceptives, and it broke during sex… oh, I don't know. I'm grasping at possible reasons. To me it adds up, but then I'm not a copper. Surely you can see how plausible that could be, can't you?"

"Of course I can. Even if your line of thinking is accurate, Heather, it's not an offence to have an affair."

"Then what are you doing wasting time here? You should be out there, looking for evidence to capture the man guilty of *killing* my daughter."

"I understand you being upset, Heather. I want to assure you that my intention is to keep questioning the suspects we have already highlighted, in the hope that one of them will finally fold and admit to the crime. Do you know when the funeral is going to take place?" Sally asked, changing the subject, wishing to cool down Heather's anger a little.

"The *funerals,* you mean? No, the Whiting family have so far kept me out of the loop there," she replied bitterly.

"I can ring Mark if you like. Would that help?"

"No. They'll probably think I've put you up to it. I'm sure they'll tell me eventually, once the arrangements have been made."

"Very well. We'll be going now then. I'm sorry to drop such a devastating bombshell on you. I want you to be assured that I am doing everything I can to bring your daughter's killer to justice."

"I'll have to take your word on that, Inspector," Heather said once they'd reached the front door.

Sally smiled at the woman, but Heather slammed the door in her face in response. "Well, that could have gone better."

Back in the car, Joanna locked her seatbelt in place and said, "Let's hope she doesn't go around there to cause a stink."

"Do you think I was wrong, telling her about the pregnancy?"

"No. I think she had a right to know. However, looking at things from her point of view, boss, I know I would want to avenge my daughter and her child's death."

"Really?" Sally was shocked to hear the constable reveal that. "But without evidence, there's little we can do to place Colin at the murder scene."

"Maybe you should call him in for questioning for his own sake then. It's pretty obvious she has him in her sights as being the father of the child."

"Rather than let Heather get her hands on him? You think she'd be capable of harming him?"

Joanna shrugged. "I'm not a mother, and neither are you, boss. Who's to say how we would feel in the same situation? A mother's love is a powerful force to be reckoned with, or so I've been led to believe. She also intimated that she has a temper on her at times."

Sally started the car and pulled away from the kerb. She headed back to the station but changed direction when she was halfway there. "Maybe I'll do as you suggested and bring Colin in, after all."

Colin Whiting was standing in his drive, watering a hanging basket, when Sally and Joanna walked up the path. "Hello, Colin."

"Inspector? What brings you out here?" he asked in a hushed voice.

"Is your wife inside?"

"She is. Why?"

"Tell her you won't be long. I'd like you to come to the station for more questioning."

He placed the watering can on the ground beside him, and through gritted teeth, he said, "What? I've told you everything I know. Why are you harassing me?"

Sally laughed. "It's hardly police harassment when I'm asking you politely to accompany me to the station, Mr. Whiting. I'll even let you have a solicitor this time. How's that?"

"Are you saying that I need one? Why?"

"Let's discuss that back at the station, shall we?"

"But I'm due at work in a few hours."

"I'd suggest you ring your firm and ask them to get someone to cover your shift. I can't express enough how important it is that I question you further today. Now, we're wasting time. Do you have a number for a solicitor, or do you wish me to appoint the duty one when we get to the station?"

"I have one. Let me get my coat and explain to Leona what's going on."

"You have five minutes, Mr. Whiting."

Sally and Joanna kicked stones off the path while they waited for Colin to reappear. Leona peered out the living room window and glared at Sally when she waved at the woman. "Oops, someone's not pleased to see me."

"Right. I'm ready." Colin pulled on his black waterproof jacket and pressed the key fob to open his car. "I can take my own car, yes?"

"Of course. You can drop the attitude during the drive to the station, too, Mr. Whiting—unless you have something to hide, that is."

"If I have an attitude, Inspector, it's because you've turned up at my home unannounced and unexpected, when all I've done is abide by your wishes and been honest with you."

"Good. Then you have nothing to worry about. Honesty is always the best policy in these circumstances. Don't you agree, Constable?"

"Wholeheartedly, Inspector, especially if someone can prove their innocence."

Colin opened his car door and scowled at them. "I *have* proved my innocence. Look where it's got me. My solicitor will wipe the floor with you; I can guarantee that."

"Follow me, if you will, Mr. Whiting. I'd hate for you to get pulled over for speeding on the way."

He huffed and jumped into his car.

CHAPTER TWELVE

Sally watched Colin Whiting's fury escalate as he waited in the reception area of the station for his solicitor to arrive.

A dishevelled man in his early forties entered the room and shook Whiting's hand.

"I'm DI Parker, if you'd like to come with me."

"Mr. Scottman. Sorry for the delay, Inspector."

Sally accepted his apology then led the way up the grey corridor.

Joanna and a uniformed officer were already present in the room. Sally started the tape and introduced everyone.

"Thank you once again for taking time out of your busy schedule to drop by for questioning today, Mr. Whiting. I really appreciate your cooperation in this matter."

"According to my client, Inspector, you have already questioned him in connection to his sister-in-law's untimely death. May I ask why you've dragged him in here a second time in as many days?"

"We don't make a habit of it, I assure you, Mr. Scottman. Our time is valuable, especially at the beginning of an important case such as this. However, it would be foolish of me to ignore a significant piece of evidence that has come our way since our last meeting."

"Which is?" both men asked in unison.

"That the deceased was pregnant when she died."

Colin's features darkened, and he reclined in his chair and folded his arms. "So... oh, I get it! This is why you wanted a DNA sample from me."

"Actually, it wasn't. That was to eliminate you from the crime scene. However, I did ask the pathologist to run the test, all the same, and bingo bongo, what did he come up with?"

"Are you saying the child was mine?"

Sally suppressed the urge to applaud him. "You don't seem that surprised, Mr. Whiting. Why is that?"

"Then your radar is way off, Inspector. This piece of news couldn't have come as more of a shock to me."

Sally thought back to the conversation she'd had with him at his house, in front of his wife. She clicked her fingers. "That's right. Your wife told us that you're in the process of going through fertility tests."

"I wasn't referring to my personal life."

"This whole situation is about your *personal* life, Mr. Whiting. Have you fathered any children before?"

"No. What has that got to do with anything?"

"Just asking the question. How do you think your wife is going to react when she hears the news?"

He huffed out a breath and tightened his arms in front of him. "No doubt she'll be over the moon! How the *fuck* do you think she's going to react?" He sneered, revealing a side of him that Sally hadn't witnessed before.

Scottman glanced at his client and shook his head.

"What?" Colin snapped at his brief. "Have you never heard a client utter the word *fuck* before?"

Scottman kept his head down and stared at his notebook.

"Well, at least it's answered one question for you during the fertility process."

"Nice, Inspector, very sensitive," Colin bit back.

"It wasn't meant as a derogatory slight on your wife. I was merely stating a fact that you could possibly pass the information on to the fertility clinic," Sally pointed out with the tightest of smiles.

"Duly noted. So does this put me at the very top of your list of suspects?"

"I'm afraid it does. It also gives us a prime motive, too—as I'm sure Mr. Scottman will attest to."

"Well?" Colin asked his brief.

"It certainly highlights a motive; the Inspector is right there. However, I doubt very much the fact that you fathered a child with the deceased could be regarded as a *prime* motive."

Sally looked at Scottman as if he were a crazed lunatic. "Seriously? You really believe that?"

"I do, and I would do my utmost to challenge that fact if this ever goes to court, Inspector."

"Okay, then I guess you and I obviously view the damning evidence differently."

Scottman looked up from his notebook and nodded, ending the conversation.

"So, in view of the *damning* evidence against you, Mr. Whiting, are you willing to tell me what kind of relationship you had with your sister-in-law, Gemma Whiting? Bearing in mind that I'm also aware of some kind of argument you had with the deceased at a family barbecue in August of this year." Sally couldn't help feeling smug when Scottman sharply turned to face his client.

Colin waved away the solicitor's concerns. "It was nothing."

Sally frowned. "What? The relationship?"

"The *argument*."

"Why don't you disclose what it was about and let *me* be the judge of that. Did this occur before or after your affair ended with the deceased?"

"After, and it wasn't really an affair, Inspector. Sorry to throw water on your enthusiasm."

"Then what would you call it?"

Colin shrugged and stared at Sally as he struggled to supply a suitable answer.

Sally suddenly remembered that he'd had a sexual assault charge against him. "Or perhaps it was something more sinister altogether?"

He narrowed his eyes, and his jaw moved as if he were grinding his teeth. "Meaning?"

"Maybe you did have an affair, in your *mind*. Perhaps you *forced* Gemma to have sex with you."

His eyes widened, and colour rose in his cheeks. "What? Are you crazy? She was my sister-in-law, damn you!"

"Funny how you're only just recognising that fact now, Mr. Whiting. If you did have an affair with Gemma, why wouldn't the fact that she was your relative through marriage have prevented that from going ahead in the first place? It's a little late playing the family-member card now, don't you think?"

"No. I had consensual sex with Gemma. I'm telling you the truth, I swear."

"Again, I only have your word on that. I also can't discount your previous conviction for sexual assault, so you'll have to forgive me there. So, how are we going to get out of this stalemate, Mr. Whiting?"

"How the fuck should I know? All I can tell you is that whatever warped suggestions you're trying to make about my relationship with Gemma, you're way off the mark. I'd also like to say, on the record, that I think the more you're looking in my direction, the less likely you are to track down the real killer."

"In your opinion."

"Yes, in *my* opinion. This is utter bullshit, and you're just grasping at straws. So what, if Gemma was expecting my baby? So *effing* what?"

"And do you think both your wife and your brother will be saying that once they learn the truth?"

He inhaled heavily. His glare intensified, and he tightened his arms once more.

Get out of that one, matey!

Still, he remained silent.

"What, not even a 'no comment'?"

His gaze continued to bore into hers.

"Not even that, eh? Okay, then I think I need to start searching through Gemma's personal effects, such as her e-mails and if she kept a diary she wrote in every day. That kind of evidence would be hard to dispute, yes?"

"You need to do what you have to do, Inspector. I'll say this for the final time: I had nothing to do with Gemma's death, and forgive me if I'm wrong, but I believe you are barking up the wrong tree. You have no evidence placing me at the murder scene. How's that for an accurate summary of your case against me?"

Sally smiled. "You're smart, Mr. Whiting. But I have to tell you that even smart suspects slip up eventually. I'd like to put this on record that when that day arrives, I'll take extreme pleasure in slapping the cuffs on you."

If she thought her comment would trip him up and force him to reconsider, she was very much mistaken. The glare he'd fixed on her was replaced by a smug smile and a wink.

Realising the suspect had the better of her, Sally drew the interview to a halt and asked Joanna to see Colin and his solicitor out of the station while she returned to the incident room, where she kicked out at the nearest chair, sending it crashing into the wall.

"We have to find it… the one clue that will nail that bastard."

"I take it the questioning didn't go well, boss?" Jordan asked warily.

"No, it didn't. There must be something we're missing here. I've just threatened Colin Whiting that I'm going to search Gemma's personal effects in the hope he might show some apprehension at the prospect—he didn't."

"Maybe he was bluffing," Jordan suggested as Joanna walked into the room.

"What's your opinion of him, Joanna? Do you think he's telling the truth?"

"You'd have more experience about that than me, boss. To me, he seemed innocent, but what do I know?" Joanna shrugged.

"Mind if I interrupt, boss?" Stuart asked.

"Go on."

Stuart looked down at his notes. "While you were interviewing Colin Whiting, a Miss Nadine Thornley called to speak to you."

"The name sounds familiar. What about?"

"It should. She's one of Gemma's friends who went out with her that night. We haven't got around to speaking to her yet because she's been working away. She's some kind of sales rep. I've got her address if you want to drop by."

"I take it she knows something that she thinks we should be aware of."

"Could be. She sounded a bit upset on the phone. Otherwise, I would have suggested she comes to the station to see you."

"Sounds intriguing. Come on, Joanna. Let's go for a ride, see what Miss Thornley has to say."

Sally rang the bell to the new block of swish apartments.

The door was opened almost immediately by a pretty brunette wearing a concerned smile. "Are you the police?"

"We are. I'm DI Sally Parker, and my partner is DC Joanna Tryst. I believe you have some information you'd like to share about Gemma Whiting, Miss Thornley?"

"It's Nadine." She opened the door to let them in. "We'll go in the lounge."

Once they were all seated on the two cream leather sofas, Sally asked, "First of all, I'd like to express my condolences. Did your friends inform you of Gemma's death?"

"Yes, Audrey left me a message on my answerphone. I lost my mobile a week ago and haven't had the chance to replace it yet. I was devastated when I heard what had happened. Gemma was such a lovely person. Have you arrested anyone yet?"

"No, we're still going through a list of suspects. Sorry to be so blunt. My colleague said that you might have some valuable information for us."

"I've hardly slept last night since hearing the news. Audrey said what kind of questions the police had asked her, and I've been mulling things over during the night."

"Okay, take your time," Sally said once she saw the tears welling up in Nadine's eyes.

"Melinda was one of Gemma's closest friends. Unfortunately, she died a few months back through cancer."

"Yes, I'm aware of that. Tragic news."

"It was, to all of us, especially Gemma. After the funeral, I noticed a change in Gemma. Of course we were all really upset by our friend's death, but it appeared to hit Gemma strangely for some reason."

"Can you enlighten us as to how, Nadine?"

"Yes, she was hit as hard as all of us, but she recovered swiftly. She seemed much chirpier in herself after a few days' grief, and I just couldn't figure out why, so I came right out and asked her."

"And what was her response?"

"She told me that it was as if a beacon of hope had gone off in her head the minute Melinda had passed. She assured me that she was distraught by Mel's death, but it had given her the strength to alter her own way of thinking."

"Strange. Thinking about what?"

"She meant her marriage. I know she and Mark haven't really been getting along properly as man and wife—if you know what I mean?—for a few months now."

"I see. Did Gemma have any love interests outside of the marriage?"

Nadine gasped and covered her chest with her splayed-out hand. "No. She wasn't the type to have an affair."

Sally glanced sideways at Joanna, hoping that her partner wouldn't display any reaction to the news. She didn't. "All right. Did she confide in you in which way this sudden strength would reveal itself?"

"She did. She told me that she had been applying for jobs out of the area."

"So, you're telling me that she had every intention of leaving her husband?"

"Yes, it was just a matter of time. She needed to find a way of securing her future first, before she said farewell to her past."

"Do you know if she was successful in her search to find a job?"

"I got the impression she had been, but when the realisation struck, she stopped talking about it. Maybe she thought I'd let it slip to Mark. I wouldn't have, but who's to say how people react when they're on the verge of turning not only their own lives upside down, but also that of those around them. She was very protective of Samantha, wanted the transition to be as smooth as possible to avoid upsetting her daughter too much."

"That's fair enough. Can I ask if you know what went wrong in the marriage?"

"Are you asking if Mark was ever violent towards Gemma?"

"I suppose that's exactly what I meant. Was he?"

Nadine rubbed the side of her face as she thought. "Gemma didn't mention anything to me. When I asked why she wasn't willing to stick with her marriage and give it another go, she seemed quite evasive."

"In what way?" Sally asked.

"I can't tell you. She never confided in me that much, and I didn't like to push her."

"Interesting. Do you happen to know where Gemma was searching for jobs? Was it her intention to leave the area?"

"Yes. The London area, I believe."

"That's quite a trek. Is there anything else she mentioned in passing that you can recall?"

Nadine chewed her lip then shook her head. "No, not that I can think of."

"One last question before we go. Did Mark's brother, Colin, ever crop up in conversation?"

Nadine contemplated the question a few seconds then shook her head. "Again, I don't recall her mentioning him, except in passing."

"In passing?"

"You know, when he showed up at a family gathering with his wife, that sort of thing."

"I see. Well, you've been really helpful. I'm sorry for your loss."

"Thank you. I hope you catch the person who did this. I always thought this was a safe area to live in, Inspector. Times really are changing, aren't they?"

By this time, the three women had reached the front door of the small flat. "They are, unfortunately. Put it this way: our jobs are definitely getting harder to conduct."

"Good luck."

The door closed quietly behind Sally and Joanna.

"I think we need to drop by and see Mark, don't you?" Sally said.

"I think so. It's all rather intriguing, isn't it?"

"You're not wrong there, Joanna."

CHAPTER THIRTEEN

When Sally parked outside the Whiting family home, the last thing she expected to see was Colin's car parked in the drive. As Sally left her vehicle, she was alarmed to hear raised voices coming from inside the house, as well as the distinctive sound of a woman and child screaming.

"Shit! Quick, Joanna, call for backup."

Sally left her partner and ran down the side of the property to the back gate. She pushed it open and rushed through the courtyard garden and in the door that led to the kitchen. Following the voices, she barged into the lounge, where the two brothers were tussling with each other. She rushed in and eased her way between them, pushing a hand into each man's chest. "All right, break it up, you two."

The men withdrew a few feet and scowled at each other.

"Thank God you arrived," Yvette cried out. She was holding Samantha behind her back, shielding the child from the fighting men.

"What's going on here?" Sally demanded. She remained between the men in case they started to fight again. Both of them had cuts to their faces; Mark had a split lip, and Colin's eyebrow was dripping blood. Neither of them would tell her what the kerfuffle was about. She tried again. "If I have to drag you both down to the station to get it out of you, I bloody will. Now what's going on?" Testosterone was emanating from the pores of both men as they locked gazes with each other through slits in their eyes. Yet neither one of them was willing to freely admit to Sally why they had been fighting each other. Sally turned to the men's mother and inclined her head. "Yvette, are you willing to divulge what this is about?"

"I think you should tell Colin to leave. He's caused enough trouble as it is."

"I will, once I've heard what's been going on," Sally replied harshly.

A breathless Joanna entered the room. "Backup is on the way, boss."

"There, did you hear that? Now, speak." Sally's head swivelled between the two men, each appearing to have calmed down a touch, if only momentarily. "Yvette, maybe it would be better if you and Samantha left the room."

Joanna escorted the distraught woman and her granddaughter from the room, and Sally took a step back to see if the two men could be trusted not to attack each other. "Why don't we all take a seat and calmly discuss this, like adults? Surely you can see how much this is upsetting your mother and Samantha?"

Mark was the first to relinquish his angry gaze. He heaved out a breath and sat down on the easy chair in the corner. Sally turned to face Colin. With a raised eyebrow, she motioned for him to sit on the sofa. Then she moved over to the fireplace, leaned against the mantelpiece, and folded her arms. "Who wants to go first?"

Neither man responded.

"Colin, why don't you tell me why you're here?"

"All I did was come round and ask when the funeral was, and he started hitting me. I have no idea why."

"Is that true, Mark?" Sally asked.

Mark Whiting's head dropped. His chest rose and fell rhythmically as he tried to control his breathing. "Yes, it's true. You'd beat the crap out of him, too, if you'd learned what I had today."

"Which is?" Sally looked over at Colin, who was intently avoiding eye contact with her.

"Mum told me there was something going on between him and Gemma. I wanted to know what she meant by that, and he blurted out that Gemma was expecting his bloody child. Don't tell me you wouldn't have reacted the same way, Inspector, if you'd been hit with that bombshell."

"I'm sorry you had to hear the news like this."

His eyes widened as he stared at Sally in disbelief. "*You knew?*"

"Yes, the information has only come to my attention within the last few hours. I asked Colin to come down to the station to give me an insight into his relationship with your wife, but didn't get very far. I take it you had no idea this was going on, Mark?"

He flew out of his chair and paced the carpet in front of him. "Of course I bloody didn't. I knew there was something wrong with Gemma but didn't have a clue she was shagging my brother behind my back. I don't know who I'm more disgusted with—him or her! Well, it'll have to be him because she's no longer here, but you get my drift. Is that why you killed her, you cheating bastard?"

Colin's lip curled. "You're out of your mind, Mark. I didn't frigging kill her. I *loved* her…"

Mark's arms spread out to the side and slapped hard against his thighs. "This just gets better and effing better."

"Why don't you both calm down?" Sally intervened.

"*Calm* down! Are you having a bloody laugh? I want him arrested."

"For what?" Sally asked, unfolding her arms in readiness in case things became heated once more.

"For a start, for impregnating my missus. And for another, that act could be deemed a motive for killing her, couldn't it?"

"*I'll* do the detective work, if you don't mind, Mr. Whiting. For your information, having an affair is not an arrestable offence in the eyes of the law."

"Well, it bloody well should be, especially when one of the adulterers has lost their life in suspicious circumstances."

Colin nodded. "Maybe you're right, bro. Only the spotlight should be pointed at *you*, not me."

"What? Are you bloody insane? I loved Gemma. What the hell are you insinuating?"

Sally held back for a moment, letting the men's war of words take shape before she tackled anything they revealed.

"Well, she clearly didn't love you. Why would she have sought comfort from me if she loved you?" Colin taunted in anger.

"The mind boggles, especially with your past record. Do you know about the sexual harassment case my dear brother got done for, Inspector?"

Sally nodded. "Yes, and I've questioned Colin at length about his previous conviction. I would have been foolish to ignore it. But I have to say, Mark, I was on my way over here to ask permission to look through Gemma's computer and diary, if she had access to either of those two items."

His brow furrowed. "Why?"

"I need to chase up another piece of vital information that has come my way this afternoon. If you refuse, I will get a warrant to remove these items if they exist."

"Why would I refuse? I don't understand. I want my wife's murderer found as much as anyone else. I still think it's him," Mark said vehemently, pointing at Colin.

"Don't be absurd, man. Give her the laptop and diary. Maybe that'll prove how much she loved *me* and not you."

Mark charged at his brother. Sally tried to separate them but struggled. "Joanna, get in here!"

Joanna barged into the living room with two uniformed officers close behind her. Sally stepped back and ordered the PCs to pull the men apart. "Take Colin Whiting out of the room." Once Colin had been removed from the room, Sally pointed at the sofa. "Sit, Mark. I need to ask you a few questions."

Looking bewildered, he dropped onto the edge of the seat. "What did I do? You expect me to just take that crap from him?"

Sally sat at the other end of the sofa with Joanna standing by the closed door. "No, I don't. But fighting with him isn't going to solve anything either, is it? Right, now that he's out of the room, why don't you tell me what it's been like living with Gemma these last few months?"

"Hard. But that still doesn't mean I would go out and kill her, if that's your next question."

"It wasn't, but thanks for the clarification. Why didn't you tell me when we first met that your marriage was having difficulties?"

He shrugged. "I genuinely didn't think we were in that much trouble. Doesn't every relationship go through fraught patches?"

"I suppose so. Will you give me access to the items?"

"Of course. I have nothing, and I mean *nothing* to hide."

"Thank you, I really appreciate that. Can you get the computer and diary for me now?"

Mark left the room and returned carrying the two items a few moments later. "What is it you're looking for?"

"I need to check on some information gathered today which could be crucial to the case."

"Sounds all very secretive. Am I allowed to know what that information is, Inspector?"

"In time, Mr. Whiting. I'll give you a receipt for the items. Any idea when Gemma's funeral will be?"

"Her body is being released to the funeral home today. I need to go down there and arrange everything with them. I'm not sure if I'm up to it just yet. It's hard to say farewell to a loved one, no matter what evidence you might find in there to the contrary," he said, pointing at the personal belongings he'd just given Sally.

"I don't doubt that. If you can let me know, I'd like to attend the funeral, if time permits."

"Wouldn't your time be better spent searching for the murderer? If you're positive Colin is innocent."

"In our experience, we like to show up at the funeral in case the killer decides to lurk. It's not unknown."

"Really? Why? To gloat about the crime he's committed?"

"In a way. Some get a kick out of observing the pain and suffering they've caused to the victim's family and friends."

"That's sick."

Sally nodded her agreement. "It is. Very common, unfortunately."

He returned to his seat and placed his head in his hands. "I still can't believe she's gone. Samantha has had nightmares every night since Gemma left us. How do you tell a five-year-old sensitive child that her mother will never walk through the door again?"

Sally tutted. "You mean you haven't told her yet?"

He shook his head and looked her in the eye. "I can't. I've gone part-time at work so that I can be here more for her. Mum does her best to help out. She keeps telling me that I should grow some balls—to 'man up,' if you like—and tell her. It's easier said than done, though."

"I'm sorry that you find yourself in such an untenable position, but you're going to have to tell her sooner or later. She has a right to know the truth."

"What? That someone killed her beautiful mother intentionally? Can you imagine how you would react if you heard those words at her young age?"

"I can't. But for both your sakes, you need to sit her down and tell her the truth so that you can get on with your lives. You've said that you've gone part-time. Do you mind telling me how you can afford to do that, Mark?"

"The insurance money."

Sally and Joanna exchanged shocked glances but said nothing. That piece of news put Mark Whiting further in the frame for being a major suspect.

"I see. What about the house? Is that paid for now?"

"Yes, the mortgage will be paid off as part of the life insurance package. We're secure in that respect. Are there any more questions, Inspector? I'd like to see how my child is after the upset Colin caused her earlier."

"One last question, if I may?"

"Of course."

Sally smiled. "Going back to the state of your marriage—were things between you serious enough that either of you had mentioned the *D* word?"

"Divorce? No, never. Personally, I didn't think things were that bad at all. Has someone told you otherwise? Did Colin suggest that?"

"No. I was simply asking the question. Maybe reading Gemma's personal notes will uncover more than we're expecting. Good luck telling Samantha about her mother's death."

"Thank you. What will happen about Colin?"

"I'll get my boys to escort him off the premises and warn him of his future conduct. Although I doubt you'll be able to prevent him showing up at the funeral. Maybe it would be better if you tried to sort things out beforehand."

"By that, I take it you think he's innocent?"

Sally acquiesced. "I really don't believe he's guilty of anything more than falling in love with the wrong person. Sorry if that's not what you want to hear right now." She patted the laptop and diary. "Let's keep thinking that way until we find proof otherwise. I honestly don't think he's guilty of killing Gemma. There's no clear indication of any evidence at the scene suggesting he carried out the attack."

"Do you have any evidence linking any suspects to the crime scene, Inspector?" he asked, hope lingering in his tired eyes.

"No. It's all rather puzzling at present. We'll keep digging until we find something. I can assure you of that."

"Please keep me informed."

"Of course, if you'll try and stay out of trouble as far as your brother is concerned."

"I will."

Sally, Joanna, and Mark walked through the house to the kitchen. Yvette was sitting at the kitchen table, feeding her granddaughter triangle sandwiches. Sally's heart skipped a few beats as she studied the girl sadly. Her eyes drifted up to Yvette's. The woman smiled tautly at Sally, and she couldn't tell if it was the grandmother's way of holding back threatening tears or what. Either way, she smiled and exited the back door with Joanna.

Outside, Colin Whiting was resting against the back door of his car, with his arms crossed. "Am I in trouble?"

Sally marched up to him and pointed. "Pull any smartarse stunts like that in the future, and without hesitation, I'll whisk you off to the police cells and bang you up for the night."

"Whoa, what the heck did I do?"

"It really is pointless talking to you, isn't it, Mr. Whiting? Everyone else is in the wrong, bar you. I'm right, aren't I?"

"All I know, Inspector, is that their marriage was on the rocks, hence her seeking solace in my arms. What more is there to say?"

"Tell me, are you convinced that Gemma was about to leave Mark for you? Is that it?"

"Maybe." He shrugged nonchalantly.

Sally snorted. "I think I have recently found out something that majorly disputes that, but please, do continue to live in your dream world. You seem to take pleasure in that."

"Well, don't stop there," he ordered, his eyes bulging like a bullfrog's.

"Actually, I think I'll do just that. Always good for an investigating officer to have something up her sleeve she can whip out when least expected. Enjoy the rest of your day, Colin. I'm sure I'll be in touch with you again soon."

He grumbled and snatched his car door open and jumped in. His tyres squealed when he pulled out of the drive. Amused, Sally sniggered. "I think I've pissed him off."

Joanna opened her car door and motioned with her head back towards the house. "She seems pretty hacked off, too."

Sally looked over her shoulder. Yvette Whiting was standing at the window. Her focus remained on Colin as he drove away until the vehicle was no longer visible. Only then did she turn to look at Sally. The woman seemed flustered by their attention and swiftly bustled away from the window. "Hmm... must be hard on her, trying to referee her sons and keep her granddaughter out of harm's way at the same time. Then there's the funeral to arrange. I, for one, wouldn't swap places with her; that's for sure."

CHAPTER FOURTEEN

Sally sat at the spare desk next to Joanna so that it was easier to compare notes as they searched through Gemma's diary and laptop. She booted up the computer and went directly to Gemma's 'sent e-mails' folder. The last e-mail Gemma had sent was on the day of her murder. It was in response to an e-mail from an accountancy firm in London, which had offered her a full-time job with a very generous salary.

"Interesting. Joanna, when was the final entry Gemma made in her diary?"

Joanna flicked through the pages of the small diary and tapped her finger. "The day before her death."

"Read it out to me."

"Life begins again soon... if all goes well tomorrow. There will be no stopping me... or should I say us."

"That's it?" Sally asked. Joanna nodded. "I wonder who the 'us' is."

Joanna hitched a shoulder. "Could be her daughter or maybe a man friend. Perhaps she had plans to run off with Colin."

Sally tutted. "I'm not so sure. I think the relationship was one-sided. I get the impression he was clinging to her. This image of them having an argument at the family barbecue keeps jumping up and down, vying for attention in my mind."

"Perhaps the argument was about her dumping him for another man," Joanna offered.

"Go back to when the barbecue occurred. See if she highlighted that incident at all. If we can find out what that little set-to was about, maybe, just maybe, we'll find the break we've been searching for."

Joanna hurriedly turned the pages. "This is what she wrote on that day: *"Colin still won't take no for an answer. Not sure I can take much more of him constantly hounding me. If he persists, I'll have to tell Leona."*

"Tell Leona what, though?" Sally muttered thoughtfully. "That they had an affair, or the fact he wouldn't stop pestering her?"

"It is puzzling. Would it do any good bringing him back in for questioning? In light of this evidence?" Joanna asked.

"That's just it, what do we have really? Nothing, except proof of a lover's tiff."

"It does highlight that there was an issue between Colin and Gemma though, boss."

"Yes, but without solid evidence, no court will entertain such inadequate findings. I'm at a loss to know what to do next. Let's keep trying to find something significant to wave under Colin's nose." Sally's mobile rang. "Hello, Jack. I've been thinking of you all. How's it going?"

"Hi, boss. It's going. The baby is hanging in there, a determined little treasure, like her mother. However, the doctor has just informed us that he thinks we should consider christening her in case her condition deteriorates."

"Oh, shit! That doesn't sound good, Jack. How's Teresa doing?"

"She's walking around in a daze right now, pacing the family waiting area, crying in fits and starts. If I could take away the pain that's hounding her, I would in a heartbeat."

"I know, it must be difficult watching her being torn apart like that. Try and stay positive, love. The little mite has lasted this long when the odds were stacked against her."

"Thanks, boss. Just what I needed to hear, as always. How are things going with the investigation?"

"Nice change of subject there, partner. I get your drift. I think I'm more confused than ever about things. At the moment, Joanna and I are ploughing through Gemma's diary and laptop to see if that throws up something we can grasp. It's all getting a little tedious. You know how these things are. Without any evidence as such to latch on to, we're up shit creek."

"What about the other girl who was attacked? Any links there?" Jack asked.

"No. Her attacker turned out to be black."

"So? You're adamant that the murderer is connected with the family. What if he isn't?"

"I'm going with my gut instinct on this one, Jack. Nothing is going to sway me on that, either. This family is full of shitty secrets. Hopefully, one of them will make a major slip-up soon to help us out. Until that transpires, we'll just keep digging."

"Well, good luck. Sounds like you're going to need it. I better go. Donna's giving me the evil eye."

"Keep in touch. Give everyone a hug from all of us here."

Jack hung up.

Sally squinted to see through her tired, sore eyes as she continued to sift through Gemma's e-mails. To Sally's amazement, Gemma had never exchanged a single e-mail with Colin. She voiced her concern to Joanna.

"Maybe they were deleted. Either by Gemma or someone else since her death."

Sally nodded. "You could be on to something there. I've not found anything of note except about the job proposal, so I think I'll hand it over to forensics, see what they can find out through the computer's history." She picked up the landline and dialled the pathologist's number. "Hello, Simon. It's Sally Parker. I'm glad I've caught you."

"Inspector. What can I do for you?"

"I was hoping you'd ask that. I have in my possession Gemma Whiting's laptop. I wondered if I dropped it over, whether your expert would have a spare few minutes to go through the e-mails and see if anything had been deleted recently?"

"You're suggesting this might have happened after the victim's death, as in the murderer covering up his connection to the victim?"

"That's exactly what I'm suggesting. Any chance you can rush it through for me?"

Simon groaned. "If you drop it over this evening, I'll get one of the lads on it first thing. How's that?"

"You're an absolute star. I don't care what others say about you." Sally chuckled.

"Now I know you're winding me up. Mr. Obliging, that's me, within reason of course."

"Don't ever change, Simon, you're a treasure for sure."

"Yeah, that should be buried. Go on, say it! Twist the knife—you usually do."

"Simon! Really, you have such a low opinion of me."

"I'd say I have a pretty accurate opinion of you, Inspector."

"Seriously, I'll drop by and see you in an hour or so, once I've finished here," Sally said cheerily.

"See you then."

She hung up. "Joanna, can I have a look through the diary?" She held out her hand, and the constable placed the closed book in her palm.

"My pleasure, boss. I don't think you'll find much in there, but be my guest."

After half an hour of trying to decipher a few cryptic clues written by Gemma's hand, Sally was inclined to agree with the constable.

"Okay, let's call it a day and start afresh tomorrow, people. Bright and early, all right?"

Sally dropped the laptop off at the lab then drove to her parents' home. The first thing she did when she arrived at the house was grab Dex's lead and take him for a long walk to clear her tired mind. *What am I missing? What is someone deliberately hiding from me to deter me from picking up the scent?* "Oh well, Dex, I'm sure all will be revealed soon enough, boy. Here, go fetch the Frisbee." She threw the fluorescent-pink ring, and the excited dog barked at the toy as it skimmed through the air then floated to the ground about fifty feet away, along the river bank.

The frustrations of the day were replaced by apprehensive thoughts of her impending trial against Darryl. She hoped the photographic evidence she had supplied of the last beating he'd dealt her would be enough to convince the judge to come down on her side. Nevertheless, there was always a lingering nugget of doubt, burrowing deep beneath the surface, that was willing to remind her that he had 'respected and honourable' friends in high places, whom he could rely on to give him a stunning character witness should the need arise.

I'll find out soon enough. There's no point dwelling on things now.

She returned home and spent a fun-filled evening with her parents, playing the card game Sevens for a low stake of a pile of pennies. Of course, her father won, just as he always did. In reality, Sally was feeling generous enough to let him win.

CHAPTER FIFTEEN

March 2016 – six months later.

Sally tapped her partner on the shoulder as she walked through the incident room. "Come on, my treat. Let's grab a coffee and a doughnut in the canteen."

Jack was out of his chair quicker than he would have been if a lion had zeroed in on his scent. "Who am I to turn down such generosity?"

Once they were halfway through their doughnuts, Sally raised the subject of Jack's granddaughter, Mary Rose. "You haven't said how Mary Rose is getting on lately. Is she doing okay?"

His eyes glistened with love. "Yes. She's growing stronger every day. Still under the doctor's care, of course, but they're monitoring her from a distance now."

"That's wonderful news, Jack. You guys deserve a break. She's been to hell and back—you all have this year."

"She's definitely a fighter. How are you bearing up? Any sign of that shithead lately? I bet he's kept his distance now you're back home."

"Nope, as far as I know, he's still doing his debt to society, picking up litter in his spare time." Sally looked down at her cup of coffee and pushed her doughnut away.

"Can you believe that piece of dog turd got one hundred hours of community service? I know I frigging can't. It's bloody outrageous, if you ask me."

"I suppose he must've stashed away more of 'our' money than I gave him credit for because the barrister he employed probably cost a small fortune."

"The system is screwed up when bastards like that get away with…"

Sally reached over and patted his hand. "You can say it, beating the crap out of a woman."

"Yeah, well, it's true. Christ, if ever there was a circumstance where vigilante justice could or should be justified, it's with your ex. I'd love to track him down and string him up by the balls."

Sally chuckled as the image inspired by her partner's cruelty ran through her mind. "In all honesty, Jack, the cretin isn't worth it."

"I know. If ever he bothers you again, though, tell me, won't you? I won't hesitate to knock some sense into that twisted, warped brain of his. How did the move go at the weekend? All settled back into your folks' home now?"

"Yep, it took a while to sort out the mortgage arrangements, but we finally got there. Everyone, including Dex, seems far happier. Mum and Dad have even started having a sneaky cuddle again. They used to be under so much stress, it took a toll on their ability to show affection towards each other."

"That's great to hear. Hate the thought of couples coming up to retirement age being snowed under with bills they can't meet. It just ain't right, is it? You all right?"

Sally was distracted, leaning sideways, listening to a conversation going on between a couple of uniformed officers at the next table. She raised her hand and placed a finger to her lips to silence her partner. After hearing a certain person's name a few more times, she finally had to say something. "Sorry, I don't wish to appear rude, but would you mind telling me why you've just mentioned Mark Whiting's name?"

The young female constable shrugged. "I had to sit with him at the hospital while his wife died."

Sally's brow creased sharply, and she looked over at her partner, who appeared to be equally confused. She turned back to the constable. "Wife? When did this happen?"

"Last night, ma'am."

"What? We are talking about Mark Whiting of Chapel Grove in Easton, aren't we?"

"That's the one, ma'am. Do you know him? I'm sorry if you thought I was being disrespectful talking about the incident."

Sally waved away the apology. "Nonsense. So you're telling me his wife had some kind of accident and died of her injuries. Is that correct?"

"Yes, ma'am. At her home. He came home and found her lying in a pool of blood yesterday about six. An ambulance was called, and they rushed her to hospital, but it was far too late. The blows Kathy received to her head crushed her skull. She never stood a chance."

"Why hasn't this case come through to us?" Sally asked Jack.

"No idea. This is incomprehensible. We need to get over there ASAP."

Sally scraped her chair back and smiled at the constable. "Thanks for the information."

Jack ran after her as she blazed an infuriated trail through the station back to her office. "We should have been informed, Jack."

"I agree. Anything to do with that family should be flagged."

Sally asked Joanna to pull up the incident report on her computer screen as Sally brought the team up to speed on what had just transpired.

"Whoa, yep, here it is. It must have slipped through the net, boss. The initial report has it down as a burglary gone wrong."

"I want the investigating officer's name, Joanna. Get him on the phone immediately."

Joanna looked up the details and dialled the number. She handed the phone over to Sally once she'd been connected to the detective constable in charge of the case.

"Dave Jarvis, I'm DI Sally Parker. Do you have a minute to come and see me? Sorry, that came out wrong. This is not a request—it's an order. My office, immediately!"

Five minutes later, Sally's irritation had grown exponentially while she waited for Constable Jarvis to put in an appearance.

Eventually, a wide-eyed young man barged through the door, wearing a troubled frown. "Ma'am? You wanted to see me?"

"My office, now. Jack, join us, will you?" Sally tried her hardest to keep her anger under control, but she could feel it bubbling beneath the surface. She took a couple of deep breaths and threw herself into the chair behind her desk. "Take a seat, Jarvis."

"Have I done something wrong, ma'am? You seem pretty hacked off about something."

"That's putting it mildly. I'm not going to take a glitch in the system out on you, Jarvis. It's true; I'm more than a little pissed off right now. Tell me about the incident you attended last night."

"The burglary, ma'am?"

"No, the fatality. See, that's what I'm having trouble getting my head around. Why on earth haven't you reported this incident to this department? Correct me if I'm wrong, but I thought we were the Murder Investigation Team for this station."

"I'm sorry, ma'am. I was going to do it when I came on shift. I only came on at two, came in to a pile of stuff to attend to on my desk, and to be honest, contacting you slipped my mind."

"*Slipped* your mind?" she asked incredulously.

He scratched his head and looked suitably embarrassed by his foul-up. "You know what it's like, ma'am. The pressures of the job and the time restraints we're under to meet our targets…"

Sally raised her hand as heat filled her cheeks. "Stop! Stop right there, Jarvis. You know damn well as soon as your crime escalated from a 'normal burglary', you should have passed it over, even if that meant you going into a few minutes of overtime. Am I right?"

"Yes, ma'am. I apologise, but it was my wedding anniversary yesterday, and the wife had booked a table at a restaurant in town and…"

Sally shook her head. "I don't want to hear it, Jarvis. Your inability to police a case properly has probably aided a criminal's escape. Is that fact lost on you?"

"No, ma'am. Again, I can only apologise. There have been a few spates of burglaries around that area, but we don't have any DNA evidence pointing us in any firm direction."

"I'm not bothered about the burglary aspect to this case, Jarvis. Are you not aware of a serious crime we investigated six months ago, concerning Mr. Whiting?"

He shook his head.

"Then let me fill you in. Mr. Whiting's wife, Gemma Whiting, was beaten and left to die on a country road not far from the family home."

"Shit! Sorry for my use of language. Did you catch the culprit who carried out the attack, ma'am?"

"No, unfortunately there was no DNA found at the scene, and out of the two main suspects, we couldn't decide which one carried out the crime."

"Two suspects, ma'am?"

"Yes. One was Mr. Mark Whiting, and the other was his brother, Colin Whiting. The case is still ongoing, and anything relating to that case—i.e., other incidents involving the family members— *should* have been reported to this team *pronto*. Now do you understand why I'm so livid?"

"Totally understand. I'm so—"

"Sorry. Yes, I know. Apologising isn't going to help us solve these crimes, though, is it?"

The constable's shoulders slumped.

It took Sally considerable strength not to feel sorry for him. "What's done is done. Did Mr. Whiting happen to mention how long he'd been married to Kathy?"

"He was too devastated to really hold a conversation with me, ma'am. I thought it best not to push him for answers at the time, you know, because of his grief."

"Because of your anniversary dinner, you mean?"

He tried to counter her accusation, but Sally raised another hand to suppress any lingering objection.

"Was Whiting alone at the hospital?"

"Yes, ma'am. When I arrived at the house, the crime scene, he was there, obviously along with his mother and his daughter. Both were extremely distraught by what had taken place. I accompanied Mr. Whiting alone to the hospital."

"I see. So you haven't had the chance to really question the mother then? What about the victim's relatives? Have you contacted them?"

"No. I was planning on going back out there today to question Mr. Whiting's mother, when time permitted. As for Mrs. Whiting's next of kin, I think Mr. Whiting took care of that. He rang them from the hospital."

"That one sentence tells me that you had no real intention of handing the case over to us as you previously suggested, Jarvis. You need to get your story straight, man. As for *thinking* someone has already done your job for you, well..." Sally had heard enough. Evidently, if she needed to know anything about the case, she would need to take control of the investigation herself. "Jack, do me a favour and escort Mr. Jarvis out of the office."

"Yes, boss." Jack tapped the detective on the shoulder and motioned for him to leave the office. "Come on, son."

"You're making me out to be the criminal here. I find that grossly unfair and offensive, if you don't mind me saying, ma'am," the constable blustered as he stood up, ready to follow Jack.

"I'm doing nothing of the sort. There are specific procedures in place for us to follow, which you clearly have neglected to do. I suggest you take the matter higher if you think I have misread the situation. But I think you'll find any complaint you raise against me will be regarded as trivial, once you share how inept you've been in the case so far."

Jack winked at her and left the room with the constable. She took her shoe off and threw it at the door once it was closed. Retrieving her shoe, she picked up the phone and rang the pathology department. "Simon, it's DI Sally Parker."

"Hello, Inspector. It's been a few months since we last spoke. What can I do for you?"

"I'm assuming the body hasn't arrived yet."

"Body? Any *body* in particular?"

"A Mrs. Kathy Whiting."

"Not yet. Why does that name sound familiar?"

"As in the *second* wife of Mr. Mark Whiting, the deceased Gemma Whiting's husband."

"Really? He remarried, and now the second wife is also dead?"

"That pretty much sums it up in a nutshell, Simon. I'll need your guys to go out to the scene. This time, the murder took place inside the marital home."

"When did this occur, Inspector?"

"Around sixish last night."

"Okay, here's a very obvious question for you. Why am I just hearing about this case now?"

"Precisely. Don't ask. Put it down to incompetent policing by a constable—not on my team, I hasten to add. He's been ripped to shreds, I can assure you. Anyway, the poor woman died from her injuries in hospital last night. Can I ask you to prioritise the PM for me?"

"Of course. I'll get on to the hospital after our call is over and chase up the corpse. Maybe this will mean you can finally conclude Gemma's case and bang Mark Whiting up for good."

"Yeah, that's what I'm hoping, too. Shame we couldn't have done it before he took another life. If he's guilty, that is."

"I believe that it's going to be hard for him to persuade you otherwise."

"I'm on my way out to the house to see Whiting now."

"I'll send a team out when one becomes available, Inspector. Good luck, I'll get the report back to you sharpish, once I've carried out the post."

"I appreciate it, Simon."

CHAPTER SIXTEEN

Two cars were parked behind one another in the drive when Sally and Jack arrived at Whiting's house.

"Looks like he's got company," Jack noted as they walked up the path to the front door.

Sally rang the bell.

Seconds later, Mark Whiting opened the door. He looked shocked to see them. "What are you doing here?"

"Mind if we come in for a word, Mr. Whiting? It's in connection with the crime that was reported last night."

Mark wrenched open the door, and it clattered against the wall. Sally and Jack followed the disgruntled man through to the kitchen. Mark sat at the kitchen table next to his mother and daughter.

"Hello, Mrs. Whiting, nice to see you again. Sorry it's under difficult circumstances once more."

"Inspector. This is a very sad time for all of us. Can't your questions wait twenty-four hours?"

"I'm sorry. No, they can't. Can I ask you and Samantha to leave the room while we have a chat with Mark?"

Yvette glared at her for a split second then shrugged reluctantly and grasped her granddaughter's hand. "Come on, Samantha. Let's see where Teddy's got to, eh?"

"Yes, Grandma. I think he fell under the bed last night. I forgot to pick him up. Poor thing has been in the dark all night."

"We'll go and rescue him," Yvette said as they left the room, closing the kitchen door behind them.

Sally and Jack sat down in the chairs vacated by Yvette and her granddaughter. Jack took out his notebook and pen then waited for Sally to ask the questions.

"Why don't you tell us what happened here last night, Mark?"

He placed his head in his hands and ran them back and forth through his short hair. His eyes looked sore, as if he'd spent the night crying. The scene didn't really touch Sally, though—she'd been subjected to numerous displays of play-acting over the years. "I told the constable who showed up here last night."

"Did he take down a statement?"

"No. I wouldn't have done it anyway. My priority was getting my wife to hospital for the care she needed to keep her alive. Lot of good that did her," Mark replied, his voice quavering a little.

"Okay, I'd like you to run through the events of last night. What time did you get home?"

"I was at work until five forty. I got home just before six o'clock."

"Where did you find your wife?"

"In the lounge. Do you want me to show you?"

"Later. Was there anyone else in the house when you got home?"

"Yes, Mum was in the lounge. She was in shock. I found her staring at the body."

Sally raised an eyebrow. "And yet it was you who called the police. Is that right?"

"Yes, she was too traumatised to do anything, Inspector."

"We'll need to speak to your mother, in that case, as she was the one who discovered your wife. Did she say how long it had been since she'd found Kathy?"

"A matter of minutes, I think. Like I say, she was too shocked to say or do anything."

"I see. She seems okay today."

"I suppose she's come to terms with Kathy's death. She's been a tower of strength to me, caring for Samantha while I was at the hospital last night."

"That's what mothers do, Mark, in circumstances such as this. Why was your mother here last night? Does she live with you now?"

"No. I'm not sure why she was here, to be honest. She's here most of the time. Never needs an excuse to pop round to see her grandchild. She's an integral part of our family life. Both Kathy and I work full time, and Mum cares for Samantha after school most nights."

"That's reassuring to have childcare on tap like that. So what time did Kathy come home from work?"

"About five fifteen. She worked as a secretary at the local school. She's never later than that."

"Did your mother see her attacker?"

"No. She said she was in the kitchen, fixing dinner. She heard shouting and things crashing on the floor not long after Kathy returned home and then silence. Mum ran into the lounge to find Kathy lying in a pool of blood and the front door wide open."

"Hence you thinking that a burglar had entered your home? I have to say that it's very rare that burglars attack people, in our experience."

"What if she disturbed him in the act? Wouldn't he lash out before he took off?"

"Probably, but then not enough to kill someone. They usually worry about their escape before hitting attack mode. There again, we could be looking at a whole different breed of burglar here. So, you walked in a few minutes later. Is that correct?"

"Approximately five minutes later. The first thing I did was check to see if Kathy was breathing, then I rang for an ambulance. Mum was still traumatised when the paramedics turned up about ten minutes later."

"Could you see the injuries Kathy had suffered? Or did the doctor say what injuries had occurred?"

"She was beaten around the head mostly. The blood was everywhere. I got covered when I hugged her to me. You should see the walls and the ceiling—it's everywhere. Thank God Mum ordered Samantha to stay in her room." He swallowed hard, and tears welled up in his eyes.

"We'll see for ourselves soon enough. I've instructed a team of Scenes of Crime Officers to join us. They'll need to search for DNA evidence, of course."

"Of course. When can we start clearing up?"

"Seems a strange thing to ask, Mark," Sally retorted quickly.

"I have a five-year-old daughter, Inspector. I was hoping life could return to normal swiftly for her sake. I'm sorry, maybe that was selfish of me to say that. Kathy meant the world to me. My mind is all over the place."

Sally tilted her head. On one hand, she could understand his reasoning. On the other, she had never come across a victim's partner openly suggesting they wanted to get their lives back to 'normal' immediately. It seemed very odd for him to even voice such an idea, and even odder for him to tack on the last part, which sounded as if it had been for their benefit. "I see. I can understand that." Sally felt Jack's eyes boring into her from the side. She tapped his foot with hers under the table and watched out of the corner of her eye as his gaze returned to his notebook.

"Will we have to move out?"

"Yes, for the time being. At least until the SOCO have completed gathering evidence. That's not a problem, is it?"

"No. Mum will have us. Is there anything else? Only, I better go and pack a bag for Samantha and me."

"That's all for now, I think. Oh, wait a minute. I'll need Kathy's parents' details, address, and phone number. We'll visit them after we leave here."

"Why? Why do you have to get them involved?"

Sally's frown matched Mark's. "I don't understand why you would ask that, Mr. Whiting?"

"They've been through enough lately, what with losing their son in a car crash last month."

Sally nodded as things cleared in her mind. "Ah… is that why you delayed telling them at the hospital last night?"

"Yes. I tend to put others' feelings before my own, Inspector."

"I'd still like their details. It's our duty to inform the relatives about an ongoing enquiry and the direction it will take," she stated, hoping the fib wouldn't raise his suspicions too much.

He left the table, went over to the dresser drawer and removed a small address book. After opening it to the appropriate page, he handed the book to Jack.

"Thanks," Jack said once he'd noted down the information.

"What's next? Us moving out?"

"Yes, that will be the next step. I'd like a word with your mother. Do you think she's up to it?"

"I can ask her. I'll swap places, go and look after my daughter and send her in, if that's okay?"

"Great stuff."

The instant Mark left the room, Jack leaned over and said in a hushed voice, "Bit odd what he said about clearing up the mess quickly, wasn't it?"

"You spotted that, eh? Hmm… it's all sounding very strange to me, and I can't put my finger on why. It's as though Kathy's being here was some kind of intrusion—an inconvenience, even. He seems upset enough, but we've seen some award-winning displays of fake emotions over the years, haven't we?"

"We have. I'm inclined to think…" Jack stopped talking as the door eased open, then Yvette Whiting entered the room.

"Hello, Yvette. Come in. Are you up to going over the events of yesterday? I'll make it as brief as I can."

"If I must. Your timing could be better, Inspector. We've all lost someone very dear to us."

"I know. The sooner we get the investigation underway, the more likely it is that we'll arrest the culprit. You can appreciate that, yes?"

"I can. What do you want to know?"

"Please take a seat."

Yvette sat opposite Sally and Jack and began twisting a tissue through her fingers that she was staring down at. "What can I tell you that Mark hasn't already told you, Inspector?"

"We'll see. As Mark wasn't on the premises at the time of the incident and you were, probably a lot. Why don't you tell us in your own words what happened?"

One of her hands brushed across her brow before she plucked up the courage to speak. "Kathy left me and Samantha in the kitchen to make a telephone call to her boss. The next thing I know, she shouted at someone, and I heard a lot of things crashing to the ground."

"That must have been terrifying for both you and Samantha. What did you do next?"

"It was. I was in a desperate quandary. After a few moments' hesitation, I ran upstairs with Samantha and locked her in her room, fearing for her safety. When I came down, I rushed into the lounge to see what was going on."

"That was brave of you. Can I ask why you didn't stay upstairs with your granddaughter?"

She paused for a second then replied, "Because I wanted to do all I could to help Kathy."

"That's very admirable of you. When you entered the lounge, was the intruder still present?"

"No. I found Kathy lying on the floor."

"Mark said that you were traumatised. Did you approach Kathy at all? To see if she was conscious?"

"No. I froze on the spot. Mark came home a little while later. He dealt with her then. Called for the ambulance, took control of the situation."

"I can't imagine how you must have felt, seeing your daughter-in-law's life in the balance like that."

"It was truly awful. I was at a loss what to do. I was so thankful when Mark came home and relieved me of the responsibility."

"How is Samantha?"

"She keeps asking for Kathy, which is understandable."

"Mark told us they were very close."

"Since her real mother died, Samantha has clung to Kathy as if she were her own flesh and blood."

"I hear that you've been helping out the family, too, looking after Samantha while Kathy and Mark were at work."

Yvette looked Sally in the eye and nodded. "It's what close families do, isn't it, Inspector? Watch out for each other."

"Not always. And you got on well with Kathy?"

"Of course. She was a lovely girl. Anyone who takes on a grieving man and his active five-year-old daughter must be a very special person indeed, wouldn't you say?"

"I would. What a shame she has been snatched from the bosom of this family, especially as she was loved by you all. How on earth is Samantha going to cope now? Losing two 'mothers' within six months of each other?"

"She'll cope. I'll ensure that happens. Don't you worry," Yvette snapped, as if Sally had questioned the family's ability to care for the grieving child.

"I'm sorry. It was merely a question. It wasn't meant to cast any aspersions as to anyone's inabilities to combat the stressful situation."

"We'll cope. We're a close-knit family who has overcome far more than this over the years and come out the other side unscathed."

"Glad to hear it. When you're feeling up to it, I'd like you to make a statement. Is that okay?"

"Yes, can you leave it a few days? Let me get over the shock of losing Kathy."

"Of course. One last question before we wrap this up. How was Mark and Kathy's relationship? Sorry, how long have they been married?"

"One month to the day. They were newlyweds; how do you think their relationship was?" she retorted harshly, almost as if Sally had asked an insulting question, which couldn't have been farther from the truth.

"How terrible. Now your son has to go through the grieving process all over again."

"He'll do it. He has a very strong resolve, Inspector."

"Tell me, as a matter of interest, have you seen much of Colin lately?"

She gasped. "Colin? You think he did this?"

"Whoa, no, I said nothing of the sort. Only six months ago, I turned up here and had to separate the fighting brothers. I was just enquiring, in a roundabout way, if the brothers had made amends with each other after they fell out."

"I see. Yes, he came to the wedding. We haven't really seen anything of him since then. He was very distant at the wedding. I think he and Leona are going through a tough time right now."

"Any reason why? The fertility problems, maybe?" Sally suggested.

"In a way, yes. Leona found out that Gemma was expecting Colin's child, and she went ballistic."

"Did *someone* let that fact slip intentionally?" Sally asked, with one eyebrow raised.

"Certainly not! At least I don't think so."

"Are you going to tell me who that someone was, Yvette?"

Her eyes narrowed as their gazes met. "It was Kathy who let it slip. Are you suggesting that you think Leona might have killed Kathy now?"

"The idea never even occurred to me, but now you've mentioned it, it would be unwise for me to ignore. We'll definitely be broadening our nets because of the information you have provided."

"Is that all, Inspector? I'd like to get back to caring for my distressed grandchild now."

"Yes, that's all. We'll need you to give us a statement in the next day or two, though."

Yvette nodded, rose from the table and left the room without saying another word.

Jack leaned closer and whispered, "What is it with this family? Looks like everyone has the knives out and is willing to embed them into each other's backs."

"That's an excellent assessment, Jack. One that I fear is going to make our job very difficult over the coming days or weeks."

"What's your initial take on what you've heard so far?"

"Let's discuss that when we leave here," Sally said, winking.

Mark returned to the kitchen as Sally and Jack were tucking their chairs back under the table. "Are you leaving now?"

"Yes, we're going to head over to Kathy's parents. Before we go, something is puzzling me, Mark."

His brow furrowed. "What's that, Inspector?"

"The fact you married so soon after losing Gemma."

He shrugged. "Because I was lonely, I guess."

"Did you love Kathy?"

His eyes widened. "Of course I loved Kathy. I hope you find the person who killed her soon."

"I have a feeling we will this time, Mr. Whiting. We'll be in the area for the next few days, conducting house-to-house enquiries with your neighbours."

"You say that as though I should be worried about what you obtain from my neighbours."

"Not at all. Just informing you of what is going to take place within your area. We'll be in touch soon. In the meantime, if you can compile a list of what you think the burglar took, we'd appreciate it."

"I've had a quick look around and couldn't see that anything is missing. Maybe Kathy disturbed the burglar before he had a chance to get his hands on any of our possessions."

Sally nodded, and Mark led them into the lounge. The scene was sickening, even to Sally. Blood covered every surface from the walls to the ceiling. There wasn't a clean surface in sight. Mark showed them out of the house. Walking back up the drive, Jack muttered, "Yeah, and maybe there wasn't a burglar after all, mate."

"I think you've got it in one, partner. The problem we have now is proving or disproving that theory," Sally agreed in a hushed voice as she looked back at the house. Mark was standing on the threshold, hands deep in his pockets, watching them.

CHAPTER SEVENTEEN

Sally parked the car in Kathy's parents' drive in a quiet cul-de-sac ten minutes' drive from the Whitings' home. A woman with curly silver hair opened the front door to them. "Hello, Mrs. Cleeves? I'm DI Sally Parker, and this is my partner, DS Jack Blackman. May we speak to you for a moment about your daughter, Kathy?"

She heaved a large sigh and nodded. "Come in."

They followed her through the house to a country-style kitchen at the rear of the property, where a man of similar age was sitting, wringing his hands, at the table.

"It's the police, Dave," Mrs. Cleeves explained.

"What happened? How did my daughter lose her life last night?"

"Is it all right if we sit down?" Sally asked.

The couple nodded, and Sally and Jack settled into two of the pine chairs around the matching table.

"I'm sorry, but at this early stage, I can't really answer that, Mr. Cleeves. Did you go to the hospital last night?"

"Yes. That idiot son-in-law of mine rang us a few hours after Kathy was taken to hospital."

"Now, Dave, that's not fair. He must have been worried sick and not thinking straight. We must be thankful that he rang us at all, in the circumstances," Mrs. Cleeves stated compassionately.

Her husband huffed a breath in response and shook his head.

"I wondered if you could give me a little background information about Kathy. What I mean is, I know that she and Mark haven't been married long, but do you think a spurned ex-partner is capable of doing this to Kathy?" Sally asked tentatively.

"But we were told that a burglar broke into the house and attacked our daughter. Are you telling us that was a blatant lie, Inspector?" Mrs. Cleeves asked.

"No. We've yet to confirm that. I was merely covering all angles from the outset rather than discover the information a few weeks further down the line."

"I see. In that case, no. Our daughter has never really parted with any of her former partners on bad terms. We still can't believe that we'll never see her beautiful smile and experience her zest for life again. And after what we've just been through with her brother, too."

"I'm so sorry for your loss. Mark told us about you losing Kathy's brother recently. I hope we'll be able to share some positive news about the enquiry with you soon. Are you comfortable answering these questions now?" Sally asked.

"There's little else we can do. As next of kin, the funeral arrangements, when the time comes to make them, will be down to Mark to carry out," Mr. Cleeves said.

"I'm sure he'll be grateful for your input," Sally replied, wondering if there was a message buried in his statement. "Do you and Mark get along?"

Both of Kathy's parents nodded.

"And as far as you know, their marriage was a happy one?"

Mrs. Cleeves nodded vehemently. "Yes, they loved and cared for each other very deeply. I know they had a whirlwind romance and tied the knot within a few months of meeting each other, but they were true soulmates. Kathy loved Samantha as if she were her own. She knew from day one how much Mark thought of his daughter. It was never an issue between them. In fact, she told me only the other day that she intended to go part-time at work so she could care for Samantha properly after school, to help relieve the pressure on Yvette, Mark's mother."

"That's very admirable. A very inopportune moment for this incident to happen for all concerned then."

Mrs. Cleeves started to sob. Her husband placed a gentle arm around his wife's shoulders and hugged her to his chest. "There, there, love. Let it all out."

Sally watched the touching scene until finally Mrs. Cleeves sat upright and blew her nose on a hanky that she'd produced from the sleeve of her jumper.

"I'm sorry. I'm trying hard not to break down all the time. The thought of never seeing my daughter or my grandchild just becomes unbearable and starts me off again."

Sally reached across the table and patted the woman's hand. "I'm sure Mark won't prevent you from seeing Samantha in the future."

Mrs. Cleeves gasped, trying to catch her breath, as fresh tears trickled down her cheeks. "I know we'll still stay in touch with Samantha. But we'll never have the opportunity to say hello or cuddle our own grandchild now that Kathy has gone."

Sally turned to face Jack. He appeared as puzzled as she was by Mrs. Cleeves's statement. "Mrs. Cleeves, are you saying what I think you're saying… that Kathy was pregnant?"

"Yes, about four weeks. She told me the same time she mentioned that she was going part-time. So you see, we've not only been robbed of our beautiful daughter but also our darling grandchild."

Sally felt her heart miss several beats. She shook her head. "How devastating for you both. I was unaware of that fact. I really don't know what to say. Words don't seem appropriate in the circumstances. Look, why don't we leave this for now. Give you time to grieve and take stock of the situation."

Mr. Cleeves stood up. "Maybe that would be for the best, Inspector. Thank you for your consideration at this sorrowful time for us."

Sally and Jack smiled at Mrs. Cleeves and retraced their steps through the house, with Mr. Cleeves leading the way. "I appreciate you seeing us, Mr. Cleeves. Here's my card. Feel free to contact me night or day, should the need arise."

He took it and placed the card on the hall table close to the front door. "Thank you. Sorry we couldn't be more helpful."

"There's no need to apologise. Thank you for your time. We'll be in touch soon."

Sally heard the door close behind her and upped her pace to reach the car.

In the car, Jack let out a long whistle. "Wow! Coincidence or what?"

"Too much of a bloody coincidence for us to ignore, that's for sure. I'm going to have to run this past the chief when we get back. I think we've got enough to arrest Mark Whiting now, don't you?"

"Either him or someone else in the family who wasn't happy to hear that snippet of news."

Sally sharply turned to look at him. "Come on, let's hear it. Who do you think did it?"

"Take your pick. The husband, the brother-in-law, even the sister-in-law comes into the equation for me after hearing about the pregnancy."

"Really? Leona? Now that's one person I hadn't even thought about. Let's get back to the station and start thrashing things out before I bring the chief in on this. You've certainly got the cogs turning with that notion, Jack." Sally pointed to her forehead with one hand and started the engine with the other.

Walking through the doors to the incident room, Sally clapped to gain the team's attention. "Gather around, people. Some interesting information has come our way that we'd like to share and tear apart."

The team shuffled their chairs into position and either sat forward in the seats or armed themselves with their notebooks, ready to listen.

Sally and Jack stood on either side of the whiteboard. Jack noted down the details as Sally spoke.

"So, we turned up at Mark Whiting's house to find him, his mother, and his daughter all looking pretty shaken up by what had happened to Mark's new wife Kathy. The scene of the crime was like a clip from a horror movie. The girl never really stood a chance."

"Are you still putting this down to a burglary gone wrong, boss?" Joanna asked, tilting her head and raising a questioning eyebrow.

"The honest answer to that is, we're going to have to for now. But that's likely to change once I give the DCI the heads-up on what we've learnt from our informal chat with the members of the family and Kathy's parents.

"Okay, after we've completed this meeting, I want Stuart and Jordan to conduct house-to-house enquiries, see if anyone either heard or saw anything suspicious, like a man leaving the Whitings' premises covered in blood. There'd be no possibility of escaping the blood spray, if the spatter in the lounge was anything to go by. SOCO are on their way over there now, so we'll be awaiting their report on any evidence found. I have my doubts that they will find anything, though. Here's where things get interesting: I find it incredible to believe that Mrs. Whiting and Samantha were in the house while the burglar was attacking Kathy. How many burglaries do we come across where someone is at home to confront the intruder? Most burglars tend to cherry-pick empty homes."

The team nodded their agreement. Everyone's attention turned to the door of the incident room as DCI Mick Green entered, an unidentifiable expression creasing his features. "Update meeting, is this, Inspector?"

"Yes, sir. I was just filling in the team and allocating tasks before I came to bring you up to speed on matters."

"Saved you the bother then, haven't I? Carry on. I'm all ears." He planted his backside on the edge of one of the spare desks close to Sally and folded his arms. His eyes drifted over to the board, where Jack continued to make notes.

Sally swallowed the anxious knot that had suddenly developed in her throat. "So I'm inclined to disbelieve all this rubbish about a burglar and look at a family member committing the crime."

"And your reason for pointing the finger in that direction is?" the chief asked.

"Apart from the nonsensical angle of the burglary, we also learned that Kathy Whiting was pregnant. I've yet to get that fact confirmed by the pathologist, but I'm pretty sure we can believe Kathy's mother."

The chief seemed puzzled. "And what does that lead you to assume?"

"Well, considering Gemma Whiting died in similar circumstances, it leads me to think that Kathy was intentionally killed because of her pregnancy. I have very little else to go on."

The chief inclined his head and brought a hand up to toy with the stubble of his chin. "Interesting. It's definitely a motive. For the husband, you think?"

"Up until about half an hour ago, I would have said yes to that, sir."

"What has altered your opinion?" the chief asked.

"My partner. He raised a fair point in the car—maybe the same member of the family who killed Gemma also killed Kathy because she had just announced that she was pregnant. Seems strange that both women were killed within four weeks of conceiving. What are the odds on that?"

"What do you intend doing about it, Inspector?"

"I was going to ask you to issue an arrest warrant for Mark when I returned to the station. However, with this new information thrown into the mix, I'm in a quandary how to proceed."

"I'd yank them all in. Don't question the family at home, put them under pressure by ordering them to come to the station for an interview." The chief shrugged. "He or she who hesitates will highlight themselves as a genuine suspect."

Sally thought over his suggestion for a few more seconds before she nodded. "You might be right, sir. I'll get on the phone straight away. Ask them to come in today."

"Okay, maybe give them at least twenty-four hours to make the arrangements. Don't be too keen to point the finger at first."

"Will do. I'll ring the pathologist, see what he can tell me about the victim after we've finished. Best to have the facts in place before I start bombarding the suspects with questions."

"Always advisable." The chief stood up. "It's a shame I had to come and find you to get an update on the investigation, Inspector. See to it that doesn't happen again."

Sally seethed as she watched him walk out of the room. "See what I'm up against, you guys. Now you know why I come down hard on you now and again. Maybe you'll give me some slack on that in the future."

The team stared back at her, neither agreeing nor disagreeing.

She waved her hand in front of her face. "Never mind."

Jack cleared his throat. "So shall I draw up a list of suspects we're going to want to talk to in the next twenty-four hours?"

"Do that. I'm looking at inviting Mark, Colin, and Leona Whiting. Can anyone think of anyone else?" They all shook their heads. "Very well, let's look into all the suspects' backgrounds again, specifically pinpointing the last six months, see if anything strange crops up that we can tackle each of them with. I'll ring Simon in the meantime." Sally dismissed the team and rushed into her office to make the call. Simon's assistant answered the phone in his office and informed her that it would be another thirty minutes before he could respond to her call. Sally tackled some important paperwork while she awaited his return call.

"Inspector, how can I help?"

"Thanks for calling back, Simon. Have you had a chance to carry out the PM on Kathy Whiting yet?"

"The hospital hasn't released the body as yet. Some bureaucratic claptrap that I told them to get sorted ASAP. I have a feeling my disapproval will only make them dig their heels in even more. Why?"

"I dropped by to see Kathy's parents this morning, and they told me that their daughter had just found out she was pregnant."

"Oh, dear, how unfortunate."

"I don't think it's a coincidence, either. My money is on it being intentional, but before I go after the suspects, I need the fact verified by your good self. I know your hands are tied until you have the corpse in your possession, but as soon as you know, will you get someone to ring me?"

"Of course, even if I have to leave the PM suite myself, you will have that information ASAP. Intentional, you say? And the suspects you have in mind?"

"Yep. All members of the Whiting family. It has to be one of them, doesn't it?"

"Do you think we missed something with the first murder?"

"I have no idea. Maybe. I'm getting this niggling doubt that maybe if I'd done a better job in solving Gemma's murder, Kathy wouldn't have lost her life."

"That's being daft. How could you have known this would happen? If your assumption concerning that family is right, then the culprit is one cagey bugger. If you're intent on apportioning blame for Kathy's case, then you should put some of that blame at our door, Sally. We're the ones who struggled to find the evidence you needed to arrest the murderer. That is how it works, isn't it?"

Sally smiled. *He is such a nice man.* "Thank you, Simon. Those few words have just chased away several doubts running through my mind. I appreciate your kindness."

"Not at all. No point in apportioning blame where it's not needed. Let me breathe fire on some people down at the hospital and get you the info you need."

"You're an angel. Thank you." Sally hung up, finished off the paperwork she'd started, then rejoined her team. Everyone had their heads down, researching the family. "Found out anything of interest, Jack?"

"Nothing at all so far, boss. How do you want to play this? Are you going to ring the suspects and call them in or go round there and personally invite them to pop in to see us?"

"You think the culprit is going to do a runner, I take it?"

"The thought had occurred to me. The thing that's bugging me is why we should take the risk. You know, if the person killed Gemma and has seemingly got away with the crime, then what on earth makes someone purposefully go out and kill in exactly the same way? Surely they'd realise what suspicions that would raise, wouldn't they?"

Sally hitched up a shoulder. "Your guess is as good as mine. It only takes the minutest detail to freak a murderer out. In this case, I believe Kathy revealing her pregnancy, if that's what she did, was the trigger. Right, if nothing has shown up here, I say we head out and begin rounding them up. Let's start with Colin and Leona Whiting."

Jack rushed down the stairs of the station, trying hard to keep up with Sally's determined stride. "Hey, slow down, boss."

"Out of breath? Shame on you, Bullet." She laughed, intentionally using his ex-army nickname to enforce her point of him being unfit. She could sense him mimicking her and quickly turned to catch him in the act. "Something wrong with your nose, Jack? It's all screwed up."

He gave a slight cough and clutched the tip of his nose between his thumb and forefinger. "I have an itch, thought I was going to sneeze there for a moment."

"Hmm... I believe you."

CHAPTER EIGHTEEN

Sally and Jack arrived at Colin Whiting's home at almost four o'clock. He was outside the property, rinsing off his car with a hosepipe. He seemed surprised to see them, and not in a good way, either.

"Hello, Mr. Whiting. You seem anxious to see us. Have we come at a bad time?"

He threw the hosepipe aside and strode towards the outside tap to switch off the flowing water. "Any time you show up here, Inspector, is bad timing. What now? Someone else hit me with a harassment charge, have they?"

"Remind me to check into that when we get back to the station, Sergeant," Sally said, winking at her partner. "Actually, I'm here to deliver you and your wife an invitation."

He frowned and leaned back against the wall. "What are you frigging on about?"

"Is your wife at home? I think it best if we discuss this with both of you at the same time."

"She is. She's been under a huge amount of stress lately, Inspector. Please bear that in mind before you drop any bombshells on us."

Sally's interest was piqued. "Has she? I'm sorry to hear that. May I ask why?"

"If you must know, we're in the process of having counselling and are about to start our first course of fertility treatment."

"I see. Well, I hope that all works out for you. Shall we go in?" Sally asked.

Whiting huffed disapprovingly and grudgingly led the way into the house. "Leona, love, we have visitors."

Sally heard Leona's heels cross the wooden kitchen floor, then she appeared in the doorway, wiping her hands on a tea towel. Her smile swiftly disappeared when she recognised Sally and Jack. She turned and quickly walked back into the kitchen. Uninvited, Sally chased after her. She found Leona sitting at the kitchen table, her head buried in her hands, sobbing.

Sally raced across the room and stopped inches from the woman. "Leona, what's wrong?"

"Why? Why are you here to hassle us again?"

"Sorry? Hassle you? What gives you that impression? I haven't even said hello to you yet."

"You being in our home can only mean one thing, Inspector. You can deny it all you like, but I know where this is leading. I'm not stupid."

"Then I must be. I have no idea why you're reacting like this unless... you're guilty of something. Are you, Leona?"

Her head rose, and Sally saw confusion along with tears swimming in her eyes. "Are you telling me you're not here to arrest Colin?"

"Should I be?" Sally countered, raising an eyebrow.

"I just presumed you've finally come to arrest him for Gemma's murder. I know it's been months since we last saw you, but I'm also aware that you rarely leave a case unsolved."

"That's true." Sally looked over her shoulder at Colin, who was staring back at her in puzzlement. "Why don't you take a seat next to your wife, Colin?"

Jack followed the man into the room and stood alongside Sally. "I take it you haven't heard the news today then?"

"News? What news?" Colin demanded.

"From Mark or your mother, about Kathy."

The couple glanced at each other and shook their heads.

"No. What about Kathy?" Colin asked.

"She was attacked last night at the family home."

"What?" Colin asked, his back rigid.

"Is she all right?" Leona had the decency to ask after a long pause.

"No. I'm afraid she lost her life after she was rushed into hospital. The injuries she sustained were too much for her body to recover from."

The couple held hands. "How terrible," Leona said, shaking her head. "Poor Mark, he must be devastated. How did it happen? You said her injuries were too much. What kind of injuries?"

"Mainly to the head. Similar to the way Gemma died. Only this time, the incident took place inside the residence, not outside the home," Sally informed them, trying to gauge their reactions to the news.

Leona seemed genuinely shocked, but Colin appeared to be keeping his emotions in check.

"Similar injuries, you say? Who was at home when the incident happened? Do you know, Inspector?" Colin asked, his eyes shrinking into slits.

"Your mother and your niece, Colin." She intentionally withheld the fact that an alleged burglary had taken place.

Colin uncurled his hands from his wife's. "And Mark? Where was *he*?"

"At work."

"All right. Why don't we cut to the chase, Inspector? Why are you really here? I take it's not just to tell us about Kathy."

Sally smiled tautly. "Yes, you're right. I'm here to ask both you and your wife to accompany us to the station for questioning."

"May I ask why?" Colin asked, clear anger rising in his tone.

Sally shrugged. "Because a second major crime has been committed concerning a member of your family. Is that a strong enough reason, Mr. Whiting?"

His eyes blazed with fury. "You believe *we* have something to do with Kathy's death, the same way you accused us—or *me*—of killing Gemma? You're bloody insane, woman. What proof do you have?"

Sally held up her hands. "Whoa, now hold fire on bombarding me with accusations, Colin. All I've asked you to do is accompany us to the station for questioning. My reasoning behind that request is so that we can question you separately. Hopefully, that would help to prove your innocence. However, your overreaction is doing nothing but filling me with suspicion. Perhaps you have something to hide and are worried that you'll buckle during questioning?"

"No, you're wrong. I have nothing to hide, Inspector. Everything has to be cloak and dagger all the time with you, doesn't it?"

"Nothing of the sort. As I've already stated, we need to question you separately." She glanced at her watch. "We're wasting time. If it's all the same to you, I'd like to get the questioning completed by the end of today. Shall we go?"

Colin scoffed. "You're incredible. You haven't even asked if we have an alibi for the time the incident occurred. Is my brother being pulled in, too? My mother, what about her? She was at the scene, according to what you told us." Frustrated, he threw his arms up in the air.

"My husband does have a point, Inspector," Leona said, her eyes pleading with Sally.

"He does. But then, so do I. Okay, put it this way, if neither of you have anything to hide, then what's the harm in humouring me?"

"Because it encroaches on our basic human rights, for one thing," Colin bit back. He pointed at Sally. "Here's a novel suggestion: There are two of you and two of us. Why don't you question us here, in different rooms? How's that?" He looked up at the clock on the wall. "I have to be at work in forty-five minutes, so I don't have time to drive all the way to the station and get to work before my shift begins."

Sally turned to look at Jack. "Is that all right with you, Sergeant?" She knew he didn't enjoy questioning suspects.

Jack nodded. "If that's how you want to play it, boss."

"I'm a reasonable person, Mr. Whiting. This time, I will do as you've requested. I'll question your wife while Jack questions you. Fair enough?"

"Fine by me. Go easy on Leona, though. She's had a shock and has been under a lot of personal pressure lately." He touched the back of Leona's hand and lovingly pecked her on the cheek.

"I will; don't worry. We'll take the lounge, okay?" Sally smiled at Leona and led the way back through the house. Sally closed the door once Leona had entered the lounge. Leona sat on the sofa while Sally settled into the armchair, her notebook and pen ready for action.

"Can you tell me where you were between five and six yesterday evening, Leona?"

She thought over the question for only a second before she replied, "Here. Around that time, I was preparing dinner for a friend of mine."

"I'll need the name and contact details for that friend before I leave. And your husband? Where was he?"

"Of course. Colin had already left for work. That was around four forty-five, I believe."

"I see. Can you tell me when you last visited Kathy and Mark's home?"

"About a month ago. You're testing my memory there, Inspector. Yes, a month to five weeks ago. We haven't really been getting on since the news came out about Gemma's baby..."

"That must have come as a huge shock to you."

"It did. But Colin and I have worked through our differences and successfully come out the other side, unscathed and eager to get on with starting a family of our own." At the mention of starting a family, Leona's face lit up.

"How are things going with the fertility programme?" Sally asked, softening towards the woman.

"Slowly. It all takes time. We're keeping our fingers crossed that it'll only be a few months before they tell us we're expecting our first child. I'm trying to keep my enthusiasm restrained. I've had to deal with far too many disappointments since we started trying for a baby."

"I understand. It's always better to err on the side of caution in these matters. Were you aware that Kathy was pregnant?"

Leona's eyes widened in surprise, and her hand swept over her face. "No! Oh God, how dreadful." Then she gasped as if realising the enormity of the situation. "Gemma was pregnant when she lost her life, too. How devastating for Mark to have to deal with yet two more funerals in such a short space of time."

"Indeed. Can you tell me what Kathy and Mark's relationship was like? Was there any cause for concern there, do you think?"

She shook her head slowly. "I wouldn't like to say. As I've told you already, we've kept our distance since Gemma's death and the wedding. You don't think…?"

"Don't think what, Leona?"

"That *Mark* did this?"

"Well, it's certainly something we need to look into in light of Gemma's case still being open. Do you seriously think he would be capable of killing his wives?"

"I have no idea. It does seem strange that both women have died from similar injuries and within months of each other. Even the fact that they were both pregnant can't be ignored, can it?"

Sally wondered if Leona's comment was innocent or whether she meant to throw accusations in her brother-in-law's direction to relieve the heat from her and her husband. She wondered how Jack was getting on with Colin. "Like I say, it is something we'll be looking into. It depends what DNA evidence comes up at the scene."

Leona puffed out her cheeks, and a little breath of air escaped her lips. "Well, there's bound to be a lot pointing at Mark if the crime took place in his home."

"That's true enough. It doesn't alter the fact that there was no significant evidence found to place him at the scene of Gemma's death. Again, let's leave the speculation about that to the forensic team to sift through."

"Well, so far they haven't done a good job, if you don't mind me saying, regarding Gemma's death."

"They're still working on it. Something is bound to show up sooner or later. It always does, usually when the investigating officer least expects it. Maybe a telling connection will be made to Kathy's death. Who knows at this point? We'll be treating the crimes as separate cases until we have proof otherwise," Sally added with a shrug.

"So who really is in the frame here, Inspector? My husband and I have suitable alibis for the time of the attack."

"Well, at the moment, because of the burglary aspect to Kathy's death—"

"Burglary?"

"Yes, sorry I should have told you that. Your mother-in-law thinks that Kathy disturbed someone in the house."

"So that's why you aren't linking the crimes. I see. Is there anything else you need to ask me?"

Sally slapped her notebook shut. "No, I think we're finished now. I appreciate you taking the time to answer the questions, given the stress you're under."

Leona waved the comment away. "My husband has a tendency to overreact at times."

Sally smiled. "You don't say! If you'd like to stay in here for a few minutes, I'll just pop next door to see how my partner is getting on."

"Okay."

Sally eased the door open quietly and cocked her ear as she tiptoed along the short hallway to the kitchen. Everything seemed nice and calm between the two men. She rapped her knuckles on the door and entered the room. "Are you nearly finished?"

Jack nodded. "Just having a chat about football, boss. I think we're done here. Mr. Whiting has been very amenable."

"Glad to hear it; not about the football part," she said, frowning. "We're only trying to do our job, Colin."

"I appreciate that, Inspector. I've calmed down a lot since your arrival. My wife and I really have nothing to hide. We're regular folks just trying to live normal, stress-free lives. Although that's proving difficult to do with our involvement in the fertility treatment, as you can imagine."

"So your wife has been telling me. Stick with it; I'm sure everything will turn out for the best. Right, Sergeant, we better get back to the station. Thank you again for sparing us the time in your busy schedule, Colin."

Both Colin and Jack left the table, and then together with Sally, they made their way towards the front door where she shook hands with Colin. "I appreciate your cooperation."

"I hope you find the culprit soon, Inspector," Colin said then closed the door.

Sally and Jack jumped in the car before either of them spoke.

"Well, how did it go with Leona?" Jack asked, turning in his seat to face her.

"I think we can cross her off the suspect list. What about Colin?"

"Yeah, I'm getting the same impression. We'll need to verify he was at work when the incident happened. If that turns out to be the case, then there's little we can do to dispute it, is there?"

"Damn, just a minute." Sally shot out of the car and ran back up the path to the house.

Colin opened the door with a worried expression on his face. "Did you forget something, Inspector?"

"Yes. Your wife was going to supply me with her friend's details, the lady who came to dinner last night while you were at work."

"Ah, yes, just a second." He disappeared and returned with a piece of paper bearing the woman's name, address, and phone number.

Sally waved it and ran back to the car. "Thank you." She threw the note at Jack when she settled behind the steering wheel. "Okay, let's see what the others have come up with."

Stuart and Jordan were just getting out of their vehicle when Sally pulled into the car park. "Anything?" she asked hopefully.

Stuart shook his head. "Nothing. No one saw any sign of strangers lurking. The neighbour next door did hear a woman scream but chose to ignore it."

"Like you do," she replied sarcastically.

The four of them continued into the station and up the stairs to the incident room. Sally immediately went to the whiteboard and began jotting down notes of what the team had acquired, which amounted to very little.

"Jack, will you ring Leona's friend to check her alibi, please? Stuart, ring the bakery where Colin works to see if he was on duty at the time the incident occurred last night. Jordan, will you do the same with the butcher's where Mark works? Thanks, guys. I'll be in the office, going over the files. I have a niggling doubt we're missing something vital here."

Thirty minutes passed before her partner popped his head round the door to her office. "Just to inform you that everyone's alibi checked out, adding to our frustration."

"Grr... not what I wanted to hear. Come in, take a seat for a second."

He threw his weary frame into the chair. "How about you? Did you manage to find the clue that has been bugging you?"

"Nope. It's here somewhere. It *has* to be. I'm going to take the file home with me this evening."

"What about Mark? You think we should haul his arse in for questioning?"

"I'm going to have to run that particular scenario past the chief before I leave. We're buggered on that front if his alibi checks out."

"Maybe someone is just keen to cover his back at the butcher's." He shrugged. "I don't know; I'm just throwing it out there."

"I doubt they clock in and out at a butcher's like they do at a supermarket, so there's a possibility your suggestion is plausible. Ugh... it's all so frustrating. Two pregnant wives, two deaths. A lot of planning could have gone into this. It would be easy for Mark to bung someone a fifty to cover for him, wouldn't it?" she asked.

"We've certainly seen every trick in the book played out over the years. Why should his alibi be discounted? He's *got* to be in pole position to be our main suspect after dismissing Colin and Leona from our enquiries, hasn't he?"

She inhaled a large breath and reclined in her chair. "I have to agree with you. I wonder if SOCO asked him for his clothes."

"What he was wearing last night? Not sure that would help any. If this crime has been seriously thought out, one of the major points would be for him to cover his tracks where the deceased's blood is concerned, right?"

"You're right. It would be natural for the husband to cradle his dying wife, transferring any blood onto his own clothes in the process, either intentionally or unintentionally. But then, look at the state of the room, the blood spatter. Evidence of that would show up on his clothes, wouldn't it?" Sally picked up the phone and dialled the forensic department. "Hello. Is Simon available for a quick chat? It's DI Parker."

"He's just finishing a PM now. I'll let him know you're waiting."

"Thanks."

Both Sally and Jack drummed their fingers on the desk while waiting for the pathologist to answer the call.

"Hello, Inspector, again."

"Sorry to trouble you. It is important, I promise. When the SOCO team were at the Whiting house today, did they ask the hubby for his clothes?"

Jack mouthed something at her.

She covered the mouthpiece to the phone and asked, "What?"

Jack leaned forward. "And the mother's and daughter's clothes, while they're at it."

"Actually, my partner has just raised a fair point. Add the mother's and daughter's clothes to that question, too."

"Let me check the list of evidence they left on my desk. Hold the line."

Sally rolled her eyes up to the ceiling as she waited.

"Umm... no, they didn't. I'll be having a word with them about that. Want me to send someone back out there to get them?"

"No. Leave it to me. I have evidence bags here. I'll gather what you need and deliver them to you myself first thing. Thanks, Simon, have a good evening."

"Not much hope of that. Three car-crash victims just descended on me."

"Oops... sorry. I'll be in touch soon." She replaced the phone in its docking station and chewed on her thumbnail. "Now, do we go out there and just pick up the clothes, or do we bring Mark in for questioning tonight?"

"I don't mind putting in some overtime. Maybe run it past the chief first."

She scraped back her chair and rushed along the corridor to the chief's office. He was just leaving his office with his secretary. "Sir, glad I caught you. Can you spare me two minutes, please?"

He turned to his secretary. "You go ahead, Lyn. I'll see you in the morning."

Sally followed him into the office. "Sorry, sir. I have a dilemma that I need to run past you." She told him what was on her mind.

"I see. How sure are you that this man has committed these crimes, Inspector?"

"That's the dilemma, sir—I'm not. Everything keeps leading me to suspect Mark Whiting, though."

"Can you simply ask him to come in for questioning in that case?"

"I could. But how do I get around the issue of asking him to hand over his clothes for examination?"

The chief tutted and clicked his tongue. "Bluff it. Say that it's a usual part of an enquiry. I agree it's a tough call. If you arrest him and he turns out to be innocent, the complaints authority will drop the axe on your neck."

"Yes, sir. But then look at the evidence we have already: two wives, both recently pregnant, whether they knew it or not, killed either in the marital home or within a few hundred metres of it, at least. That can be counted as significant, surely?"

"It certainly sounds it to me. Can you place his car at the original scene, perhaps through CCTV footage or a witness account?"

"No, we never located the car involved in Gemma Whiting's murder."

"Then I think you should tread carefully. Bring him in for questioning, and this could all hinge on the clothes. If he gives you permission to examine them there, perhaps that proves his innocence. If he objects, then that should raise a red flag."

"Thank you, sir. Jack and I will head over there now. I'll let you know how things go in the morning."

"You do that. Good luck."

Sally was deep in thought when she re-entered the incident room. Something important was pricking her mind enough to make her revisit the file sitting on her desk. She flipped it open, and there it was—the infuriating missing piece of the puzzle. Her heart pounded as she raced through the incident room. "With me, Jack. Make it snappy. We've got a murderer to arrest."

CHAPTER NINETEEN

"Why? Why do you always bloody do this to me?" Jack complained, crossing his arms in the car during the journey to Mark Whiting's house.

"What? Keep you in suspense? Because I love torturing you. Honestly, your face is always a picture when I work out who the murderer is without letting you in on the secret. That, in my book, is priceless."

"You know what? Sometimes you can be as sick as some of the psychos we hunt down on a daily basis," he mumbled grumpily.

Once the car had descended into silence, Sally used the time to plan her approach. She was confident enough to go right in there and make the arrest, but she always enjoyed it when the murderers slipped up and revealed their guilt.

The same two cars from before were in the driveway when Sally pulled up at the Whiting house. She glanced sideways as she passed, a satisfied smile threatening to erupt. She kept it in check, keen not to give anything away to her partner at this stage.

Mark Whiting welcomed them, sore, red eyes the prominent feature of his pale face. "Inspector?" he gasped. "You've found him? You've discovered who the burglar—I mean, *killer* is?"

"Can we come in, Mr. Whiting?"

He pushed open the door, and Sally and Jack followed him through to the kitchen, where his mother and Samantha were reading a book together. Yvette looked up, frowning in puzzlement.

Sally smiled at the woman caring for her granddaughter. "Samantha, sweetheart, can you go and play in your room for a little bit while my partner and I talk to Daddy and Grandma?"

Samantha swept up the book and ran out of the room without uttering a word. Yvette looked miffed by Sally's interference of her precious time with her granddaughter. "Why are you here?" Yvette demanded harshly.

"Well, for a start, I've come to ask you all if you'll give me the clothes you were wearing at the time of Kathy's death?" Sally asked, giving the woman a smile.

"For what reason?" Mark asked, taking a seat next to his mother.

"Purely for evidential purposes. I received a call from SOCO, saying they had forgotten to obtain the clothes when they were here. I told them I would drop by on my way home this evening."

"Evidence? You still suspect me of carrying out these heinous crimes, don't you?" Mark asked, shaking his head in sheer disbelief.

"It's merely part of the investigation. If you object, Mark, then it will certainly raise suspicions."

"I have nothing to hide. My clothes will be full of my wife's blood because I held her, soothed her until the paramedics arrived."

"That's fine. I'll be sure to note that down. How about you, Yvette?"

"How about me *what*?" Yvette asked.

"Did you try to comfort Kathy before Mark arrived?"

"No! I was too busy caring for my granddaughter. The last thing I wanted was for her to see her step-mother in that state."

"Of course, we'll still need your clothes."

"I don't see why. I've already told you—"

"For God's sake, Mum, just do it. I don't want all this *bloody* hassle. Just give them what they want so that I can grieve in peace, for fuck's sake," Mark said, his eyes boring into his defiant mother's.

"Where are your clothes, Yvette?" Sally asked.

"Upstairs. I frequently stop over, so I keep a few spare outfits in Samantha's wardrobe. Little girls are known to be accident-prone at times, Inspector. It's always best to be prepared for such incidents."

Sally pondered why the woman would need to go into detail like that. She smiled and nodded. "Very wise. Are you intending to stay the night here with Samantha?"

"Yes, of course."

"That's great. Mark, I'd like you to accompany us to the station to answer a few more questions, if you're up to it?"

"I'm not. But if it'll help in your quest to capture the murderer quickly, then I'm willing to put myself out to help your cause."

"That's kind of you. It makes our job so much easier having compliant interviewees. One question, if I may?"

Mark inclined his head. "What's that?"

"The cream car outside, who does it belong to?" Sally's eyes left Mark and drifted sideways in his mother's direction.

"That's Mum's car. Why?"

Yvette pushed her chair back and tucked it under the table. "I'll go and get the clothes you need. They're all in the washing basket. I didn't have the heart to do the washing today. Samantha needed me."

Sally nodded and let the woman leave the room. "I don't remember your mother's car being here when we were investigating Gemma's death. Is it new?"

"I told her after the crash she had around six months ago that she should get a new car, but she insisted she wanted to keep it as it's a good runner."

"A crash, you say? Did someone run into the back of her car perhaps?" Sally asked innocently.

"No. *She* ran into the back of someone else's car."

"Oh, dear, that's a shame. Did the insurance cover the cost of repairs?"

Mark shrugged. "I can't remember. I think she covered the cost herself rather than lose her no-claims bonus."

"That makes sense." Sally heard the woman's footfall on the stairs and watched the door, waiting for her to enter. Instead, the front door creaked open. Sally's eyes widened as she stared at her partner. "Go after her, Jack."

"What? Why?" her partner asked, confused.

"Just do it! Before she gets away. Drag her back in here if you have to. Go!"

Jack bolted from the room. Sally heard a car start up on the drive and Jack shouting at the woman to get out of the car.

"What in God's name are you doing?" Mark objected, running into the hall.

"Come with me. Ask your mother to return to the house, Mark."

They ran outside to see Jack gripping the car door as the vehicle reversed off the drive. Inside the car sat a seething Yvette, with Samantha strapped into the seat beside her, looking scared.

"Mum, what are you doing? Get out of the car. Where are you taking Samantha?" Mark tried to grapple with Jack to get into the car himself, but it was pointless.

Yvette achieved her aim, reversed off the drive, and crunched into first gear.

"Stop her!" Sally shouted. Yvette's smile was akin to many evil smiles she'd witnessed from killers over the years. "Stop the car before she drives off with Samantha. Jack, use your knife. Puncture the damn tyre. Do *not* let her escape."

Jack withdrew the penknife Sally knew he kept in his waistband for emergencies and pierced a large hole in the rear tyre closest to him. It didn't prevent Yvette from driving off as Sally had predicted it would. Jack ran after the car while Sally turned to a bemused Mark. "You had no idea your mother was capable of this?"

Not taking his eyes off the car, he replied, "Do you really think I would have left my child in her care if I'd known?"

The car turned into another road, and almost immediately, Sally heard a crunching noise. She and Mark sprinted and caught up with Jack, who was staring at the two mangled cars, one of which was empty. "Jack! Are they all right? Do we need to call an ambulance? Get in there and help them! Thank God no one else was involved."

Jack tried to open the driver's door, but that was impossible, as it had concertinaed in the collision.

Mark was pounding on the passenger window. "Open this door, Mum, or I'll break the window. Let me get Samantha to safety."

The passenger door sprang open, and a sobbing Samantha shot out of the car and into her father's arms.

"Take her inside the house, Mark," Sally ordered, not wishing the girl to see what was about to happen to her grandmother.

Jack held open the passenger door and peered inside the car. "Give it up, Yvette. Taking off like that has just proven your guilt."

Yvette clambered across the front seats and emerged from the car, reaching an arm out in front of her. "Samantha, I love you. I did all this for you!"

Mark upped his pace and quickly disappeared around the corner.

"Really? You can't help yourself, can you? Even at the end, your twisted mind has to apportion the blame elsewhere. You really think your grandchild will be able to live a happy life hearing those damning words?" Sally asked the woman.

Yvette's expression was one of complete and utter confusion. "It's true. Those women wanted to take Samantha away from me. They had no *right* to do that."

"No *right*? So you thought you'd punish not only Gemma and Kathy, but their unborn children, as well. Was that the trigger? Once you found out both of them were expecting, you thought you'd punish them?"

With Yvette suddenly lost for words, her head dipped onto her chest. Sally threw her arms out to the side in frustration. "You disgust me. Jack, read her rights to her and get her out of my bloody sight."

Jack withdrew his cuffs. Sally turned and walked back towards the house to check on Mark and Samantha. When she walked into the kitchen, she found Samantha sitting on her father's lap. Both were clinging to each other, sobbing.

"You're safe now, Samantha. Daddy will look after you now," Sally said, relieved that neither of them had been harmed physically by his mother's shenanigans.

"Why? Why did she do it?" Mark asked, looking up at Sally, his eyes riddled with anguish.

"Let me get your mother to the station. I'll let her stew overnight in a cell and question her first thing. Try and get some rest. I regret thinking this was all down to you, Mark."

"What changed?" he asked.

"Something my boss said earlier about the car involved in Gemma's death. Today was the first time I've seen your mother's car. It wasn't here when we investigated the first case, so I couldn't make the connection. Obviously, I'll need to get forensics to check the car over, but even if it has been repaired, we can still find evidence to convict someone. We still have Gemma's car to match up the paintwork. Can you tell me which garage your mother uses?"

"Yes, Jenson's garage in town." He ran a hand over his daughter's face. "Do you think she would have eventually turned on me?"

Sally shrugged. "I have no idea. She is overly obsessed with Samantha for some reason. There's no telling what she would have been capable of, come the end. Try to rest now, both of you. I'll be in touch soon, okay? By the way, you might want to let your brother know what's going on, just to put his and Leona's minds at ease."

"I will. I think I have a lot of making up to do there. I know he and Gemma... well, you know. But I'm willing to forgive and forget about that and get on with our lives. Gemma's death has always been a wedge between us."

Sally smiled and nodded. "I'll be in touch soon."

She walked outside, stood on the doorstep, and sucked in a lungful of fresh air before she made her way over to the car. Sally had a feeling the journey back to the station was going to be filled with venomous remarks from Yvette, who would be more than likely keen to blame the others, rather than accept full responsibility for her despicable actions.

CHAPTER TWENTY

The following morning, Sally turned up at the station in a buoyant mood, her arms laden with copious notes which she'd jotted down overnight in preparation for the interview of Yvette Whiting that would take place first thing.

"Morning, all. Fine morning!" she announced, joyfully pushing through the doors to the incident room.

"Let's hope that mood of yours doesn't end up getting squished by Whiting. She's had a rough night, apparently," Jack warned.

"Good. Couldn't happen to a nicer person. Do you know if the solicitor has arrived yet, Jack?"

"I'll check."

"You do that. I'm going to ring the pathologist, let him know. Also, I want to see if he's carried out the post on Kathy yet." Sally marched into her office and placed the call.

Simon answered after two rings.

"Simon, I have great news for you."

"Ditto. You first," he replied.

"No, I insist, after you."

"Well, you were right. Kathy was around four weeks pregnant, give or take a few days. Now, it's your turn to share."

"We've got someone sitting in the cell for the murder of both women."

"Excellent news. Did we help you find the suspect at all?"

"Sort of. I'm relying on you to come up with the goods in the next day or two. I've got the suspect's clothes, and I've asked forensics to pick up the suspect's car. It has been repaired since Gemma's death took place, so I'm hoping it's not too late."

"If there's evidence to be found, we'll find it. May I ask who the suspect in question is, Inspector?"

"The mother-in-law of both women."

"What? Why on earth…?"

"Exactly. I've yet to question her thoroughly—I'm about to do that now. My initial understanding is that she was afraid of losing her five-year-old grandchild."

"Holy crap! So she killed the women and the unborn children out of *jealousy*?"

"So it would appear. I'll buy you a drink later this week and go over the details." Sally shook her head. *Why the hell did I say that?*

Simon chortled. "Wow, you must be excited if you're inviting me out on a date."

"Umm… on that note, I better crack on. Talk soon."

She could hear him laughing as she hung up. Her cheeks warmed as Jack appeared in the doorway of the office.

"Everything all right?" he asked.

Sally nodded. "Fine. Has the solicitor arrived?"

"Yes, indeedy!"

She slipped out of her chair and picked up her notes. "Let's get this show on the road then and see what kind of reception we get from the dear lady today."

A female PC brought the furious-looking suspect and her female solicitor into the room a few moments later. Jack started the tape and declared the relevant details.

"Right, Yvette, you seem a reasonable lady. Why don't you reiterate what you told me yesterday about the deaths of your two daughters-in-law? Why don't you tell me why and how Gemma Whiting died on the eighteenth of September, 2015?"

Yvette Whiting inhaled and exhaled a few breaths, her gaze glued to her interlocked fingers. "She was going to leave. I had to stop her."

"Leave? Leave your son?" Sally asked in a hushed voice, matching the suspect's.

"Yes. She'd been planning it for months. I found a letter lying on the kitchen table."

"What letter? Who was it from?" Sally asked.

"Her new employer—in London. I couldn't let her take Samantha away. The thought of not seeing her every day tore me apart. I had to step in and do something before it was too late."

"So you followed her home that evening?"

"Yes. She drove into town with her friends. I saw her in the garden, *flirting* with that man. How could she do that when she had a loving husband waiting for her at home?"

"So you thought you'd punish her. Is that it?" Sally asked incredulously.

"I suppose so. I was determined to prevent her running off with my granddaughter. She's my *only* grandchild. That counts for something, right?" Yvette glanced up at Sally as if seeking some kind of approval.

Sally shook her head. "No, that fact is far from being a justification, Yvette, and deep down, you know that. This is all about what is going on in your heart and your head. You've killed two innocent women because they dared to do something that didn't meet with your approval."

The woman sighed heavily. "I know I was wrong. But unless you know what it feels like to love a grandchild unconditionally, I'll ask you not to judge me, Inspector."

"I don't have to be a grandmother to know that excuse is hogwash. Why don't you tell me what occurred that evening back in September?"

"As I followed Gemma home, my blood was boiling after I saw her with him. For all I knew, she had made arrangements to meet up with this man once she'd moved to London."

"If that was true, then that would have been Gemma's business, surely?"

"She was cheating on my son—that made it *my* business," Yvette snapped back.

"Actually, she *wasn't*. Gemma and Taylor Hew met for the first time that evening. Which means you killed your daughter-in-law just because she chatted with a total stranger."

Yvette's mouth dropped open.

"So, you followed her home, then what?" Sally asked sharply.

Yvette looked sideways at her solicitor, who was frantically making notes, then Yvette's gaze dropped to her hands again. "I realised we were getting closer to her home. Something took hold of me, forced me to ram her car. I never expected her to end up in a hedge."

"Okay, I can believe that. What I can't understand is what happened next. Why don't you fill us in?"

"You have to understand the rage was bubbling inside of me. I went to the back of the car and took out the tyre wrench, or whatever it's called. She had no idea it was me. I beat her with the bar. I was shocked by the first blow, the impact it made. I couldn't stop myself hitting her. Samantha's face drifted into my mind. I got angrier and angrier, believing that I would never see my darling granddaughter again and..."

"You killed your own granddaughter's precious mother. Go on, *say* it."

"Yes. I killed her. I regretted it afterwards, once I saw the devastation it had caused to the family."

"Yet you repeated the crime only a few months later. This time, the victim was your son's second wife. In the process of that murder, you put him in the spotlight for both crimes. What kind of mother does that, Yvette?"

Her head tilted upwards, and she glared at Sally. Through clenched teeth, she said, "A *desperate* one, Inspector."

"Go on then, tell us why and how Kathy Whiting felt the wrath of your anger."

"I overheard her telling someone on the phone that she intended going part-time at work. I assumed that meant my time with Samantha would be limited in the future. I couldn't let that happen. The rage descended again. I shooed Samantha upstairs to play with her dolls and went out to the car to collect the tyre wrench again. It worked the first time. There was no reason for the outcome to be any different this time."

"What a callous woman you are. Not once thinking about how damaging your actions would be to the one you say you love most in this world. Samantha will be traumatised for life because of what you have stolen from her. How could you kill Kathy with your granddaughter upstairs in the same house?"

Tears trickled from Yvette's eyes. Sally suspected they were tears of sympathy for her own selfish sake and not for the two victims, whose lives she had ended so recklessly. "For a split second, I forgot she was even there."

"Really? You expect me to believe that when you've just told me you parcelled the girl off to her room a few seconds before?"

She shrugged. "That's how it happened. I'm telling you the truth in the hope it will ease my guilt, Inspector."

"Nice to see you showing some kind of remorse at last, Yvette. Tell me this; did you know that both women were pregnant?"

"I had an idea. If you've ever been through a pregnancy, you get a nose for these things."

Sally was appalled by the woman's admission. "And that fact didn't prevent you from reconsidering your *murderous* actions."

Yvette flinched when Sally emphasised the word *murderous*. "No. I keep telling you, you would need to put yourself in my shoes to understand the anguish I was riddled with."

"I doubt I'd ever be driven to the lengths of *killing* someone. Let alone *four* people. Because that is what this amounts to, Yvette. You've robbed this world, and your family, of four *innocent* lives."

Yvette's head dropped swiftly onto her chest as the magnitude of what she had done finally sank in. She could try to justify her actions all she liked, but the truth was there for all to see: her craziness had ripped her own family apart.

"What I don't understand is your willingness to apportion the blame on others. You had no compunction in trying to frame either of your sons. Boy, you must really hate them."

Her head snapped back up. Anger shone in her eyes. "I *love* my sons. How dare you infer that? Even after Colin did what he did to Gemma."

"What did he do, Yvette?" Sally asked, intrigued.

"They didn't have an affair. That is what he told you, isn't it? Don't make him out to be a blameless party here. It's Colin's fault that Gemma was leaving. I'm sure it was."

"What did he do?" Sally repeated with a sigh.

"He *raped* her. That child wasn't conceived out of *love*."

"What? Does Mark know about this?"

"No. We kept it a secret between ourselves. Colin being the father wouldn't have come out at all if he hadn't shown up at the house that day and opened his big mouth to Mark. I should have revealed to Mark then that I was aware that Colin had raped Gemma. My son was delusional. Colin loved Gemma so much, but she did all she could to escape his advances."

"How did you know about the rape? Did Colin admit it to you?"

"No. I was in the utility room on the day of the barbecue. No one knew I was there. I overheard Gemma warning Colin that she would tell Mark about the incident if he didn't stop harassing her."

"Why? Why didn't you intervene? Why didn't you tackle Colin about the assault?"

Yvette shrugged. "Because I had my own agenda to deal with, I suppose. During the argument, I discovered Gemma's intentions to leave Mark. She rubbed Colin's nose in it, told him that because of his actions she could no longer be a wife to her husband in the bedroom."

"And what did Colin say to that?"

"He acted like an excited puppy, thought that Gemma meant she was going to leave Mark for him."

"Wow, your family truly have a way of twisting the truth to suit their needs, don't they? That's bloody priceless."

Yvette shrugged. "I was hoping you would come down heavily on Colin, arrest him for Gemma's death, but you didn't." Yvette sneered again.

Jack nudged his knee against Sally's under the table, urging her to retaliate, "Oh, I get it—now it's our fault for not arresting the wrong person. You really are a perverse, nasty woman. Everyone is to blame but you, eh?"

"I've showed Samantha real love. She would've wanted for nothing had she come to live with me."

"You had no right to kill those women just so the access channels to your granddaughter remained open to you."

"In your opinion, Inspector."

Sally exhaled a large breath. "And the unborn children meant nothing to you, either? Is that what you're telling me?"

"No one could replace Samantha. She's an absolute treasure, the sweetest girl ever to walk the earth, and that is down to *me*. All the care and love I've shown her since the day she was born."

Sally had heard enough. She could no longer bear to be in the same room as the loathsome woman. "We're going round and round in circles here. Yvette Whiting, I am placing you under arrest for the murder of Gemma Whiting and Kathy Whiting..." Sally left the room after completing the arrest announcement under the glare of Yvette, who said nothing further in her defence.

EPILOGUE

The team met up at the pub they usually frequented to celebrate the conclusion of a case.

"Here's to our success," Jack announced, raising his pint. The others chinked their glasses against his.

Sally smiled weakly. Her mind was full of regrets for the innocent people whose lives had been affected—not only by a screwed-up grandmother, but also by her delusional son.

She doubted very much if Mark would ever fall in love with another woman, even though his mother would spend the rest of her life behind bars. He would always be wracked with guilt for what his own mother and brother had put the women he loved through. Mrs. Whiting's husband was at present recuperating in the hospital after suffering a heart attack, brought on by Sally revealing the truth about his wife. The poor man had had no idea the lengths that his wife's obsession with their granddaughter had gone to.

As for Colin Whiting, divorce was definitely on the cards for him and Leona. She'd forgiven him once for his 'affair' with Gemma. However, once Sally had disclosed the real nature of his relationship with Gemma, Leona had broken down in tears and said enough was enough as far as their marriage was concerned. Colin was, at that moment, sitting in a remand cell, awaiting trial for rape. Sally was uncertain if he would actually serve any time for his crime now that his victim was dead, but she would do all she could to see that he was punished for the crime he'd committed.

Jack clashed elbows with her. "Hey, you're miles away. You should be happy, not gloomy about this, boss. We did it."

"I know. I'm just sad for those who lost their lives. That's all. Needlessly at that. Who gives people the right to snuff out another person's life because they don't conform to their wishes?"

Jack shrugged. "Pass. At the end of the day, boss, we've done our job and caught the culprits. At least there are no recriminations on our part."

"Isn't there, Jack? Maybe not for you, but I'll always have deep regrets that I didn't arrest Yvette sooner. Maybe, just maybe, Kathy would still be with us today if we'd picked up about the car sooner. I'm off home. Enjoy the rest of your evening, everyone. See you at work bright and early, to do it all over again."

Sally left the pub and drove home. After bidding her mother and father a good evening with one of the most suffocating, loving hugs she could muster, she took Dex out for his evening walk to contemplate what lay ahead of her. Life was pretty darn good, and she envisaged it getting a whole lot better, now that Darryl had been punished and was permanently out of her life.

The end

Thank you for reading No Hiding Place; I sincerely hope you enjoyed reading this novel as much as I loved writing it.

If you liked it, please consider posting a short review as genuine feedback is what makes all the lonely hours writers spend producing their work worthwhile.

50743544R00099

Made in the USA
San Bernardino, CA
02 July 2017